DEEP

Christopher J Aggett

All rights reserved. This book or any portion thereof

May not be reproduced or used in any manner whatsoever without the express written permission of the publisher except for the use of brief quotations in a book review.

Printed in the United Kingdom

First Printing, 2019

ISBN 9781700782700

www.CJAggett.wixsite.com/Deep

I've learned that all a person has in life is family and friends. If you lose those, you have nothing, so friends and family are to be treasured more than anything else in the world.

CONTENTS

1	Tread quietly	1
2	The calm before	18
3	It's who you know	29
4	All in the balance	46
5	City streets	65
6	Play it safe	81
7	Patient 175	97
8	Operation reset	116
9	The heart breaks hard	139
10	To the hills	152
11	Eyes from above	167
12	The cabin	187

TREAD QUIETLY

My first real memories as a young girl were in the forest. Most of all I remember the mornings, the smell of pine, birds singing and the rustling of small animals under the detritus; sunlight navigating its way through trees like a labyrinth. The smell of dew and damp logs on the aga, struggling to gain momentum to bring heat to a chipped and slightly rusted off white mug sat on the hob. Its tin structure misshaped from years of abuse.

It was hard to imagine a normal life. Reading old books that were rarely available gave me a distorted impression of the world. As a young girl discovering things this way; my imagination drew up wild examples of what reality would have been like. I later found out that I was here because of my father Eli; that's not really fair although it is true I am here because of him. He was six foot two, black short hair and always serious. Never laughed or cried. He didn't talk much. He was more like an instructor than a father, spending his time teaching me how to survive. That is why I am here talking into this camera in the middle of nowhere on a mountain, alive, trying to leave something of us behind.

That cabin was my home, my school, and my prison. I must have only been around five years old. To me, that forest was a playground, a study, and a hunting ground. Those animals I used to love so much growing up became my prey. They were no longer looked at as cute and cuddly, they were food for survival. Studying everything about the modern world from a young age I learned how to survive on my own, how to survive with others and how to separate myself from the group if they were at risk. Weapon handling and marksmanship training came easy. Politics, military conflicts, and their strategies were more difficult to understand. Either way, I loved it.

When I used to ask about my mother, my father would always tell me the same story; She was a happy outgoing, beautiful person who died at a young age when I was a baby. I was too young and too fixated on my training to ask any more questions. Disappearing for days on end he would make sure there was enough wood to burn, books to read and of course plenty of jobs to do. If I wanted to eat more, then I had to go earn it, and by that I mean.... kill it. I was never very keen on this, preferring to eat from the ground instead. Learning about which plants were edible and which would leave me dying a slow and agonizing death. This went on for years. I grew more confident and gained new abilities. Mastering climbing small rock faces and making weapons from anything that could be gathered. I regularly asked my father about where he went, though he wouldn't tell me. Just that it was important and I wasn't yet in a position to understand. I assumed as I got older it was something to do with the military but never could be sure. Many times I tried to follow him without success, his tracks would always disappear; I could never work out how he managed it.

Becoming more aware as I grew up, that my father would return with random supplies; books, Cleaning materials, Weapons, and ammunition. I knew it was coming from somewhere and at the age of 19 my curiosity was growing out of control. These trips were not like his days at work. He did this in the dark of night. In the Forest where you could not see more than a foot in front of you and the noises of the animals were no longer calming, but instead intimidating. They would produce fear in a person and make them doubt their intentions, make you see things that are not there. I didn't like the night. Perhaps this is why he was more at ease with these journeys. Why he let his guard down. I always noticed that he would keep keys and money in a small wooden bowl on the table. I used to look at them and inspect them as they were unusual to me, taking such a small amount for myself that he wouldn't notice and for no other reason than my own enjoyment.

I had picked up an ultraviolet glow stick. I thought if I could get this attached to my father's clothes somewhere, then I could follow him. But that would never have worked; he was far too clever for that. He would find it too easily. So when he was asleep, I cut open the tube and poured it over the back of his pristine black leather boots. I wasn't sure if this would work but it was worth the try. As he set off for his supply run; I threw my rucksack on my back, grabbed my father's UV goggles and carefully avoided the second creaky step before quietly creeping into the night.

"Holy Shit," I said out loud to myself. "It's working"

He was roughly a hundred and fifty yards away and I was struggling to see the dull glow from the liquid as he stepped over some low laying logs. At times the glow disappeared into the ground before rising again. Looking back putting the liquid higher up, maybe on his jacket would have been better. A small mixture of panic and adrenaline washed over me as the realization of what I was doing set in.

He was moving really fast. For a big strong man, he was quick and quiet on his feet. After about twenty-five minutes of tracking him; I could see a clearing ahead of the trees. Fear of being exposed made me hesitant to move forward. I had never seen the edge of the Forest before. It always seemed so vast to me, like it was never going to end. The route we took wasn't anywhere I had been before. There were streams and small rock sections to navigate down. As I got closer to the opening I was so fixated on the lights in the distance that I missed when my father had veered off into the darkness. I didn't panic. I had found something else of interest. I pulled the goggles off and placed them into my bag, then climbed down a steep rock section; that lead onto a road.

The road ran from left to right and I couldn't believe what I was seeing. A city! In real life. It was still about a kilometre or so away and was surrounded by vast deep green mountainous forests; just like the one, I grew up in. Numerous tall buildings were scattered around the city. Lights from within glowed like fire. I could see many other small and large buildings throughout the centre. I sat in amazement taking it all in. It was incredible. Excitement consumed me, despite not knowing how I was going to make it home. My mind raced with thoughts of entering the city and it drew up wild images of the things I could find, good and bad; plus what if I got in trouble? Despite my burning desire to go; I decided to stay clear for my own safety.

To my right, I could see lights shining from a service station. A calming soft glow from inside the store crept out into the night and a bright neon light above strained my eyes. Thinking that if I go there, I would be able to run back into the forest if there was trouble, an exit route. So that's exactly what I did. Walking along the tree line until I could get close enough for a more detailed inspection. A grey truck pulled away from the storefront at speed and headed off towards the city, the gravel crunching under its tyre before gripping onto the road. I watched as it passed then looked down at the store. It was called quick trip and it was empty apart from a bored-looking girl stood behind the counter that she was casually leaning on. I could see her through the large glass window. She looked about 30/35. She too was gazing into the city, wishing she could be there.

I went in with confidence, pretending to be a customer from out of town; looking around the supplies in the shop. I couldn't believe how much chocolate was in one place. I delved my hands into my bag to see how much money I had. It wasn't much but over the years of collecting it, I had enough to buy a few things if I wanted to. I approached the girl, she smiled

"hey how are you doing. You need any help?" I felt apprehensive. I literally hadn't had a conversation with anyone apart from my father for as long as I can remember.

"No thank you, I'm good."

"Are you from out of town?" She looked me up

and down and peered outside, noticing that I didn't have a car "how did you get here? The nearest town isn't for a few hours' drive."

"OH, I walked," I said; pretending to be some lone hiker. I think she bought it.

She chuckled. I certainly looked the type with the clothes I had on. Black boots, sand colour cargo pants, and a black hooded top and rucksack. Her name badge read Sandy. Sandy? I thought. What kind of name is that? My father has always called me Dee so I suppose that wasn't much better. I looked around the store and noticed that Sandy had her eyes fixated on me. Panicked I picked up a few random bits, not even knowing what they were, and took them to the till. I awkwardly counted the change spilling it onto the counter. I was clearly nervous. Sandy probably thought she was going to be robbed. Although she wore a strange smile as if she was enjoying watching me struggle and pretend to know what I was doing. It must have been so

Deep

obvious. I collected up all of the items and dropped them carelessly into my bag. Leaving with a buzz of pure excitement, I headed back so I wouldn't be caught out by my father.

After some intense navigation, I made it home and he thankfully wasn't back before me. I placed the goggles back in his trunk and hid all my supplies under my bed and tried to go to sleep. My mind was racing, thinking of all the new things I had seen. I just wanted to go back and see more. I slowly drifted off dreaming of all the new adventures to come with my new discovery.

I was so used to eating rations; dry biscuits that you can't swallow unless you wash it down with warm water. Luxury was not something I was used to at all. So when my father would return with supplies, from what I now assume to be Quick trip, I would be so excited to try any new amazing flavours he may have brought back. Whenever I asked about them, he would always tell me that a man brings them from far away and that we can't just have things when we want them, teaching me to take my time and enjoy things. I never could. How could I when I loved the taste of chocolate so much and was denied it for so long!

The next morning I noticed my father getting ready to set out once again. I followed my routine of washing myself with odourless soap, completing my chores of cleaning the cabin and sweeping the porch that sat overlooking an eternity of trees. He was quiet as usual and hardly muttered a word before he left, this time seemingly in a hurry. I watched him leave out the corner of the kitchen window, hopping over branches and logs that lay on the ground. As soon as he was far enough away I ran excitedly into my room throwing the broom on the floor. I pulled my rucksack out from under the bed and sat with it on my lap. I pulled the heavy zip over to reveal an internal mess. Loose unorganized items half-filled its centre compartment. My hand delved in and rummaged around to find the items that I had picked up. The first thing I pulled out was a Hershey bar, my face lit up smiling ear to ear. I had had one many years ago and remembered how much I loved it. I placed it down to my side and reached into the bag again, I felt something unusual, like a small box; as I grabbed it small mysterious items inside rolled around. I wondered what it was. I pulled out an orange box with the word pieces written across the front.

"Pieces? Reese's Pieces", it was a box of peanut butter candy in a crunchy shell.

I placed that next to the Hershey bar and took one last dip into the bag of wonder. I knew that there was only one item left in there, so dug around. I pulled out some sort of packet; it was a mama Thai Curry noodles packet. My stomach rumbled at the thought of it. I had not eaten for about 16 hours and it was something I had never had before.

Deep

I rushed out to the kitchen and turned on the cooker. As a flame-licked around the bottom of the metal kettle, I found a plastic bowl and read the instructions on how to make the noodles. I placed the chocolates on the table and sat eagerly waiting for the water to boil; it seemed to take an eternity. I poured the required amount of water into the bowl and broke up the noodles with a plastic blue fork and stirred. The smell was amazing. After a while, the water had thickened up and became like soup. There was steam billowing into the air and I was ready, filling my spoon with the hot liquid, I sipped cautiously. I had never tasted such flavours; it was simply beautiful, but spicy! I wasn't used to spicy. I was eating the noodles so fast it was like I had never eaten before.

Just as I was about to take another mouthful I heard a noise from outside. My ears felt like they moved as they were alerted by the noise. Like a defence system. I looked towards the doorway and there stood my father. I felt dread in my stomach. His tall stocky frame filled the doorway in a silhouette fashion. He seemed stressed and panicked. "WHAT, what are you doing? Where the fuck did you get that form". I froze with spoon in hand; I had no idea how to reply. "WELL!" he said; his voice ripping through me. I had never seen him so animated. I knew I had really messed up this time. I muttered.

"I followed you to the store" his face dropped. He marched up to me and took the chocolates from the table and threw the bowl from under me. It flew through the door landed out the front, I could see the liquid absorb into the ground, leaving steaming noodles sat on the earth.

"NEVER follow me!" he exclaimed; "NEVER!".

I slumped back in my chair, not knowing how to react. I was not sure what was worse; his response to the situation or my devastation from having the nicest food ripped from under me and tossed away like it was garbage. He pulled his black carbon hunting bow from the rack on the wall and slammed it on the table.

"If you want to eat, go and catch your dinner. Don't come back until you do!"

I was worried; I had never seen him like this. I stood up in shock and stood in silence watching him frantically look inside a trunk in his room. He pulled out a briefcase and a holdall and looked at me. I knew something wasn't right but I couldn't speak. It was as if my voice had been stolen. He stood up tall and looking down on me. I couldn't make out his expression, maybe an apology? Instead he said nothing and left. Sweat dripped from his face as he brushed past. Then he was gone. I slumped back into my chair. The relief that it was over and the disappointment that it had happened washed over me. I stared at the noodles on the ground. They were no longer steaming. I didn't feel sad inside but instead, I felt anger. I threw my backpack on my back and

Deep

grabbed the bow, and ran outside. I ran and ran.

THE CALM BEFORE

I slowed with my legs burning and my lungs gasping for air. I dropped to my knees and struggled to calm my breathing. Looking around I realized I didn't know where I was; having never been this far before. It had been more than an hour or so since my father's outrage had dispersed. The taste of the Thai noodles was no longer in my mouth. Despite the drama that had unfolded; it was a beautiful warm day with a gentle warm breeze. The only way I learned to navigate the forest was by using the rivers, rocks and gradient to identify where I was. That is how I could tell that this was a new area for me, surrounded by unfamiliar shrubs and rocks. I climbed over a small rock section before shuffling down the other side and that's when I could see her. A beautiful doe grazing, white spots on her back and a fluffy white tail. She was stood in the middle of a beautiful meadow. The sunlight was acting as a spotlight, perfectly directing its attention to the beautiful animal. I could see all the Orange Tiger Lilies, gaillardias and black-eyed Susan's; littering the floor, the colours and the smells. I will never forget them.

As I stepped out into the meadow she saw me. She pulled her front right hoof up in the air and locked eyes with mine. I watched her for a few seconds and it felt like all of my troubles had gone away. I slowly drew my bow; my heart was beating hard as the tension made the carbon creak. I took a deep breath and held it briefly before aligning the target and slowly releasing the tension in my lungs and then the bow. The doe didn't react and as I released the arrow, it flew silently across the meadow. The arrow struck her above the heart, approximately 4-inches radius at the centre of the circulatory system and she fall gracefully away from me onto her side. I felt relief as well as a sense of calm. I walked eagerly over to her stepping over hundreds of beautiful and colourful flowers. Her breathing had already stopped. Blood had run into the earth and spoiled some of those wonderful flowers turning them into a dark red heavy mess. She was still so beautiful and graceful even in death. I braced my boot on her, next to the arrow and pulled so that I could retrieve it. I pulled so hard I flew back and hit the floor landing on my back, knocking the wind out of me. So I just lay there.

I let out a chuckle and wore a big smile as I lay in the flowers, staring at the clear blue sky that sat like an ocean between the treetops. I felt wonderful. It was so quiet and calm in the forest with such a gentle warm breeze; it felt like I was in a dream, so peaceful. I thought I would have felt bad for killing the doe, but I didn't; for so long I wouldn't do it, kill an animal, but that day was different. My father had stirred something inside of me. I felt determined. As I lay there a low rumble grew in the distance. It was quiet at first but it was getting closer and closer. My smile had gone and I sat up as my attention was rudely ripped from my experience. It was getting louder and louder until it was shaking the ground beneath me, and then two objects darkened my vision of the sky above and in a second they were gone, leaving a light white trail of smoke in its path. I felt anxious and panicked, it was a feeling that I had never felt before. What followed was the loudest noise I had ever heard. It made the earth tremble with fear; all the animals in the forest ran, Birds flew away and I gasped. It was a bomb, It must have been; I had never heard one before but had learned enough to know what it was. The feeling of dread gripped me and I knew that I had to get back, back home to the cabin, to my father. I knew he was hiding something this morning. I hope he's safe.

The sun had started to blend with the treetops; it was sinking, just like the feeling in my stomach. I could see smoke in the sky behind me, in the distance. I just knew that this was bad, really bad. There's no way that was an accident; was it military? Were we under attack? I had learned about Russian aircraft testing defences; this had been a tactic for many years but they wouldn't, would they? The dense dark green trees of the forest made the sunlight retreat too fast for comfort. With the bow in one hand and my rucksack on my back, I struggled to run home fast enough. I was bounding over fallen trees and avoiding dips in the earth. I hit a small rock with the tip of my boot as I tried to hop it. I was sent flying forwards; the rucksack slid up my back as I fell, forcing my face into a tree stump.

All I could remember was blackness. I woke up with blistering pain in my head; I put my hand on my forehead to inspect the damage. It was so dark I could hardly see anything at all; I thought the impact had made me blind. Blood had run down my face, into my eyes. It was nearly dry in some parts so I knew that quite a lot of time had passed. My eyes were sore; I did my best to wipe the blood out. I felt cold and was shaking. I knew the dangers of shock and knew that I had limited time to get home safely. I rummaged into my bag pulling a small plastic bottle of water from it; my father always made me carry spare, he said it was essential for survival.

I opened the screw top and with a shaking hand clumsily poured water onto my sleeve. So I used that to wipe the blood from my eyes; then poured the rest into my eyes and painfully blinked until I could start to see once again. I waited for my vision to return and adjust; it was a dark, dark night. It was pointless trying to move until I could do it safely. Besides, I didn't even have any sense of direction at this point. I managed to eat a few sugar cubes that were in my rucksack. I crunched them one by one, trying to prevent shock. My vision had restored to about ten yards distance and I was feeling a little more able to move effectively.

"It's time to go, Dee," I said to myself. My mind was already playing tricks on me; I was possessed by fear and found it hard to move. I tried to keep my breathing quiet but found the noise of my heart pounding in my ears. I had to move.

I navigated the darkness cautiously, each step soft and careful. The worry of what had already happened and the fear of this now uncertain time had gripped me firmly. Using my hand-wound torch only gave me a few extra yards of sight and projected a very small circle on the floor. Pointing it higher wouldn't have made a difference, as the light dissipated into darkness. It was such a black night. The moon was hidden by cloud and the thick canape ensured that no light would assist my struggle. I managed to find a section of rocks that were familiar to me. It was a stroke of luck to have done so as my torchlight briefly showed a few chalk drawings I had placed there over the years. "Yes!" I thought. I had been here so many times I could navigate it with my eyes closed, and basically had to.

It was quiet now; I couldn't hear any animals, no rustling and no explosions. Every time I stopped I almost held my breath to try and enhance my hearing. There was nothing. My head was feeling better although it was still sore, the pain inside had reduced. No more blood and I hadn't passed out with shock either, at least that was good news. It took a long time to make it home. I could see the lights from the top of the porch in between some trees. A bulb hanging bare wore a soft yellow glow, giving just enough light to guide me back in. I thankfully climbed the two wooden steps onto the porch; the door was already open. I stepped in, "HELLO," I asked with some urgency, no reply. I asked again "Hello... Eli". There was no answer; I felt worried, where is he and why wasn't he here? I could only hope he was safe and that he would return soon.

I waited for an hour and still, Eli had not returned. I cleaned myself up and inspected my injuries; I was OK, lucky really, only minor injuries. I managed to eat a few rations and hydrate while I was waiting, gaining energy was important for my recovery. I didn't know what else to do, should I go and look for him in that city? Probably not a great idea as I had no idea where to start. I had brewed a cup of tea and walked out onto the porch sipping it. Darkness still engulfed the forest; a rare appearance from the moon cast some light on the area in front of the cabin. It looked eerie. I sipped from my steaming cup of tea once more as the clouds parted; my view of the treeline ahead exposed itself. I froze instantly as the moonlight revealed a human figure lingering between trees, on the edge of the opening. The moonlight continued to fade in and out across the dark sky and the figure was no longer there. I thought the bang on my head must have been playing tricks on me.

I turned to walk back into the cabin and as I did so the hairs on the back of my neck stood up, I felt my skin tighten. A familiar noise grew in strength and at a similar rate as the fear flowed over me once more. It was the aircraft noise I had heard a few hours earlier; the noise grew and grew, until.... BANG, the explosion bigger this time. The earth trembling once again and a soft glow appeared above the trees some kilometres away. I instantly knew that I had to go, I couldn't stay here. I need to know what was going on and finding my father was the best option. I just know he is involved somehow.

Was my father safe, was I? I ran back into the cabin with some urgency, grabbing the rucksack that I had placed on the table and turned it upside down, pouring all of its random contents onto the table. Knocking over everything already placed there without concern; I upturned the bag and then put back in anything I thought would be useful, torch, food, and anything that resembled first aid supplies. I took a hunting knife I knew my father kept in his room; it was large with serrated edges and black in colour, I strapped it to my right thigh, placing the handle on the right side so I could easily access it with my stronger arm if I needed to. Only until I know I'm safe, I thought to myself. I twisted my shoulder-length brown hair, tying it up behind my head. Picked up my rucksack and strapped it on securely, took a deep breath and stepped out into uncertainty, to go into the city.

IT'S WHO YOU KNOW

The darkness still engulfed the forest, but I could see a soft glow on the horizon. Not from the explosion, that had faded fairly quickly; this looked like the sun had begun its journey back to our side of the earth. Having only been to the city that once I struggled to remember where I was going. I knew the general direction so I kept focused and stepped carefully to avoid smashing my face on a rock again. Slowly but surely I made progress. The light was beginning to reveal more and more to me as time passed but it could only be described as twilight; not light enough for clarity and not dark enough to keep my mind from playing tricks on me. I could start to see a clearing up ahead; this must be it. My fear of uncertainty grew as I climbed and the noise below got louder. I reached the top and looked down to a two-lane road, completely blocked with traffic. Men and women were shouting, and it seemed as though everyone was heading in one direction – out of the city.

I stood on the top of the rock section looking down on everyone with my bow and my blade attached to me. Not one person even acknowledged my existence. I looked to the city beyond the road; light peering over the horizon was shining bright, lighting up anything in its path. It was highlighting perfectly how the mountain enclosed the city; as if it was protecting it. I couldn't see anything unusual about it, despite all of its occupants trying to leave. I scanned to the right, further down the road; there was some sort of blockage up ahead, more people shouting, more beeping. I scanned left and could see in the distance a familiar building and sign; Quick trip. A woman got out of an orange car and her children sat still in their seats, wearing worried expressions and trying to get a better view of what was ahead.

The woman was looking concerned too; I called down to her but there was no reply. I tried again, shouted this time "HEY Excuse me!" She turned and looked at me. "What's going on?"

She looked at me blankly. "There's an emergency....we have to get out ..... We need to go, we must go". As she said this as a loud air raid siren sounded around the valley like city.

Everyone froze as the arguments and aggression were drowned out by the siren's song. She looked at me again; her face was now even more panicked as she clambered back into her car.

"You must go NOW!"

The moment of peace was brief and chaos

quickly erupted back to its previous state; the noise at the front of the barricade increased, shouting and pushing. I was still able to hear them above the siren. Two men to the right started throwing punches before falling to the floor and someone started driving into the cars; trying to force themselves out of the barricade, this situation was Mass panic. I had learnt about the dangers of it and knew nothing good was to come of it; I jumped down onto the side of the road and made a run for the quick trip, for familiar ground.

I got closer to the store noticing the morning had now broken out and the light of day shone over the city. A beautiful crisp day; perfect calm blue filled the sky above the wild city. I heard what I assumed was a gunshot from behind; my heart pounded, as I turned I could see people throwing a man to the ground and another lying on his back, he was still. I kept walking fast and as I looked beyond the hysteria, I could see smoke way beyond the city billowing up into the blue sky; the low sun shining right through it. I turned back to focus on the store, now running towards it. The traffic wasn't so bad at the store; I ran through the double glass doors that was wide open to find sandy trying to use her phone. "Answer your damn phone, pick up" her voice shaky and desperate. Items from the shelves were scattered on the floor, things were knocked over; there was a gun cabinet on the wall behind the counter with the cage open and its contents gone. "Sandy, what the hell is going on?" she turned and stared at me. The look she gave me was one of confusion, yet I was the motivation she needed to get moving

"We need to go," she said "come on" she put her phone down and walked with urgency past me, grabbing my hand along the way, Pulling me back out of the store.

"Where are we going? I need to find my father" I tried to let go of her hand, but her grip was strong and determined.

"I know a place, it should be safe," she says confidently without looking back or acknowledging my discomfort and concern.

She takes me to a grey pickup truck and told me to get in. I didn't have many options and in the chaos of that morning, safe sounded good to me. I jumped in kicking the empty and half-full bottles of Pepsi out of the footwell. I planted my feet and watched the pink fluffy dice swing as we sped away from the traffic and the store; kicking up dust high into the air as we drove aggressively mounted the road from the hard shoulder. I looked out the small rear window as we sped away, watching the people shrink into the distance. I slumped into the cold worn leather seat and looked at sandy, she focused on her driving never looking back, strangely calm and in control, wearing her brown work trousers and an equally brown polo shirt.

"Sandy, what's going on?"

"Sandy isn't my real name" She looked at me awaiting my reaction; there was a small awkward pause.

"It's Paige. There are things people don't know about this place. I'll explain it when we get there, When we're safe." She ripped her plastic badge off and threw it out of the window.

"Safe from what" I replied with eagerness and frustration.

"You don't want to know" She pushed the accelerator deeper and I sunk further into the seat and let my mind race and digest the insanity of what had just happened.

We followed the road around the edge of the city; Leading down towards the furthest end where the mountain met the buildings. Cars eagerly passed us in the opposite direction, unaware of the disruption and anarchy that they were speeding towards. We turned into the first main street of the city. Amongst the frantic energy of the street I found myself in awe of what was around me; the towering buildings casting shadows down on us. The mountainside to my right ensured that we felt very small, I was no longer looking down on the city, but looking up at it.

The more we drove into the city the more erratic the behaviour was. One group was throwing bricks through a large glass window;

glass shattered everywhere and they rushed inside before the majority of glass even had time to hit the floor.

"Fucking looters," said Paige "all they do is take for themselves .... that won't matter soon".

I looked at her with concern. What did she mean? I couldn't help but be so overwhelmed by all that was going on, I couldn't concentrate; So many experiences and emotions that I had not encountered before. I continued to take in the views; quirky little restaurants and shops, tall official buildings and a large banks with flags draped on poles that were hanging high up on their walls. The sun strained my eyes each time we passed a street that allowed it to shine through.

Nothing felt real; the sun warmed my face as I drifted in and out of a dream-like state.

"We are nearly there". I snapped back into reality as the bouncing truck moved beyond the centre of town. The buildings reduced in size and frequency as we pushed further out; solid road turning into sandy tracks, Smooth turning to rough. I could see the mountain closing us in, I must be looking at it from the other side of where I entered the city. To the right were open spaces and a few partly constructed buildings. I wound down my window to hear the siren still echoing in the distance accompanied by the constant crunching of gravel below; warm dusty air flowed into the car settling on the already dirty dashboard. We turned left onto a smaller sidetrack, the pick-up bouncing as it left more solid ground. We drove alongside a wooden fence for a few hundred yards before turning left again; I couldn't help but feel disorientated and could only see shadows ahead of us as my eyes adjusted to the darker part of the city. There were no signs, no windows, just a large grey towering building with a large metal roller door on the front.

Paige pulled up within about five feet of the entrance before sliding to a stop; the thick wheels dragging the sand and stone until we stopped, dust all around us. She reached into the glove compartment; and just as the rest of the car was full of random objects and rubbish, she pulled out a small electronic device, flipped the front up and pressed a passcode into a keypad. The roller doors in front began to lift and air from inside blew out from the ground kicking up more dust towards us. I couldn't help but think about what this place is and who exactly was Paige?

The truck pulled off crawling slowly beneath the shutters into darkness; as soon as we entered far enough the shutters began descending behind, slowly closing us in. All-natural light being reduced until there was nothing but poor lighting from plastic strip lights on the ceiling above. Paige turned the barrel on the indicator stick and the dull yellow lights poorly lit up what was in front. There wasn't a much except for a few containers and lockers. A few larger doors made of thick metal were flush with the walls and looked secure. We drove about fifty yards and slowly stopped at the other end of the small garage-like darkened area. Paige got out of the vehicle slamming the door behind as the noise bounced around the hollow room. I followed by doing the same, Paige walked past me to a door and pulled hard on the handle, it reluctantly opened with a few rusty creaks. I rummaged around in the back of the truck to grab hold of the rucksack and my bow and hurried through the door as Paige proceeded with purpose. I slammed the door behind us and followed her up a stairway.

"Hurry" Paige shouts as she speed ahead.

The stairways were dull and were aided by lights on the ceiling. Small rays of light shone through small and dirty windows too high for me to see through. We continued to go up; passing occasional doors at different levels, similar to the metal clunky door in the basement. My legs grew heavy and my head began to spin. As we got higher I tried to lean up to get a view from one of the windows, but it was no use. There were no signs and no features in the stairwell; it was like being stuck in an eternal loop and I was lagging behind Paige. Despite my fitness and time spent running through forests, I never climbed stairs like this before. I heard Paige call out to someone, alongside the familiar sound of a heavy door being pulled. I drove my burning legs up the final few steps and found a door wide open and Paige was already in the room. I stepped inside and pulled the heavy door hard towards me and it slammed shut. I turned around and stood to catch my breath; taking in what was in front of me. All along my left was an enormous glass wall running for what must have been fifty yards before turning to its right and continuing for maybe even further. To my right was a wall that only lasted a few yards. The thing that caught my attention the most was the strong smell of rich coffee; such a wonderful smell that reminded me of my home in the woods where my father and I brewed fresh coffee most mornings.

I turned the corner to see Paige hugging a woman who was slumped on the floor, a few other people sat around on random colourful chairs and some sat on leather sofas. It looked like a massive office with spectacular views around the entire city; I couldn't believe how high we were, it was simply amazing. After soaking up the view I turned back to see Paige who was upset, not wanting to interrupt I walked further into the large open space. Tables, chairs and office furniture scattered around; the odd fake plant sat on a desk, photos of peoples families and busy calendars decorated desks. All of the staff were huddled together in one corner of the room, trying to work a specific set of phones. Men in suits stood around a young fresh-faced man who sat on the floor with a laptop; all frantically trying to give the advice to resolve an issue.

Despite the chaos of what had happened and the mixed emotions of this room, something in the back of my mind was telling me to look for my father here; I looked around everyone, roughly thirty people, yet he wasn't there. They were all strangers and all of them intent on doing something with urgency; apart from one woman, she stood looking out of the window. If there was ever a face that projected worry then that was it; She peered out into the city with one arm across her chest and the other near her face as she chewed her deep red chipped fingernails. The view to the left of us was mostly mountain, behind us the same, to our right was part of the city that me and Paige had just travelled across. In front of us was the majority of the city and desert stretching beyond, as far as the blurry horizon. I could see in the distance vehicles moving around but could not tell what was going on. I softly approached the lonely woman and asked if she knew what was going on.

She turned to me "you don't know?" she looked confused and stared at me. "How did you get here?" she asked.

I instantly felt as if I shouldn't be here, like I was about to cast and wondered if I shouldn't have spoken at all. I nervously looked around and noticed more eyes had now fixated on me;

"Paige brought me"

"She's with me," Paige said with authority as she marched over grabbing my hand.

Everybody looked at her in disgust and suggested that they weren't surprised that it was Paige who had broken the rules.

Paige pulled my hand and took me to an abandoned booth.

"Sit down," she said directly.

I pulled a chair from under a desk and placed it under me; carelessly dropping my rucksack and bow down beside me.

"What the hell is going on," I asked Paige discreetly, desperately needing answers.

Paige sighed "Right, how much do you know? What has your father told you?"

I looked at her confused; "My father! You know my father?"

"Shhhhhh calm down. Yes, I know him. We work together. Well, sort of".

More confusion swept over my face. I could feel the frown on my forehead compress as she spoke. "My dad works at the shop?"

Paige chuckled "You really have no idea, do you?" She stood looking down on me.

"No really, I don't know, what the fuck is going on?"

"We need to get you to him but things have taken a turn for the worst here. Something bad has happened and we are all in danger. I can't go into too much detail, but the people here are the front of an underground operation in this city. Out there" she said pointing to the desert with an outstretched arm; "Is a military town. It is used for training and weapon experiments. You know that sort of secretive, no one should know about kind of shit. Well, put it this way. They were working on some biological experiments out there. There was always the chance that if things went wrong, then the people of this city would be doomed, trapped within its walls of rocks and trees. There is nothing else around for miles and that is precisely why it is where it is. We don't know what's happened or what the threat is but one thing we do know is that comms are down and the military is spooked. Believe me, that isn't good."

I sat there not knowing what was going on and what to make of it all. So much was going through my head and I had a feeling of dread sinking deep into my stomach.

"Ok wait, explain how do you know my

father?"

Paige stood up tall and sighed "it's complicated. I'll take you to Eli but we have to wait for the call".

"What's the call?"

"The call is from our headquarters. If there is an emergency there will be a council held in the headquarters, they will decide on the fate of this town. The problem with evacuation here is that there is only one way in and one way out. That road is the one that you saw, where the people were shooting each other trying to get out; that's the military blockade. The military will shoot anyone that tries to leave. I know this is incredibly hard to understand but they have to keep any contamination contained. The alternative is if it all goes wrong Operation Reset will be put into place, we don't want to hear that, believe me. So that is where Eli works, at the headquarters".

ALL IN THE BALANCE

Paige had continued to jump from person to person in the room, frantically talking about what options were on the table. So many different options bounced from group to group and often each idea was frustratingly dismissed. I drifted off into my own mind; conversations blended into one and some highlights of the day were eagerly dancing around in my mind. Some

time had passed by as I sat in the rc
staring out the window; swinging f
right, staring at the city streets far, far below. The streets were just as chaotic as the office. People running around, they looked so small. Nothing seemed real. A few cars were driving at speed in all directions. I snapped out of my trance and I pulled some water from my bag and drank it. I was hungry too but didn't have food to last me much longer, not to mention anyone else. I didn't know how desperate the other people here were; I thought about that for a second and pulled my bag and bow closer, Who knows how this may go.

I started to remember some advice my father gave me about people in bad situations; Trust no one, look for the exits before you need them and fight to survive. He used to say that in dire situations people would kill simply for a small amount of food or water. I put the bottle back in the bag and zipped it up. I need to be more discreet I thought to myself; suddenly feeling very vulnerable and isolated. I began looking at people in a different light; their conversations weren't just discussing options anymore, I saw them shouting and breaking down. I swung the chair back to the left and looked at the left of the city; Out towards the desert, peering high over construction sites that were deserted. In the back of my mind was constant chatter from within the room. They were no closer to fixing problems. It was as if we were shut off from the world as I peered into the distance once again. I couldn't see much but there was movement out there, in the distance. I went to find the toilet, remembering the advice that Eli had taught me I took all my things with me, after a few steps there was a loud roar and the building trembled, I peered out of the window to see another two jets fly past us, heading towards the desert. I stood still watching as my heart rate immediately increased. The jets disappeared into the distance before once again two large explosions lit up the sky and rocked the ground beneath us. Suddenly this large solid structure didn't feel so safe to me; everyone gasped and then watched in silence as a fireball rose in the distance. Seconds later it was if nothing had happened and everyone else went back to their chaotic pointless tasks. I looked around in amazement; did they not see what I did? Was I dreaming?.

I stood in the bathroom, alone. It was large, clean and looked like new. I leaned on the sink and shut my eyes for a few seconds, they stung; I don't know if was the dust, the sweat or the stress of what I had been through today. I reluctantly opened them and found myself staring back through blurry eyes.

"I look like shit".

My head was still slightly swollen and I still had blood on my face and jumper. My hands were dirty and I smelt terrible. I took my jumper off revealing my loose vest beneath and placed it next to the sink. I took the bobble out of my hair and let it hang down between my shoulders, pressed on the soap dispenser many times collecting the lavender-scented soap, using it with the warm water to wash my face and my upper body; the dirt escaping with the water down the sink as I scrubbed my arms. I dried myself off with the bathroom towels that were provided there; dirt I had not cleaned off properly spoilt their fluffy white cotton, turning them into a dark grey mess. I had never used a towel like this before; it was so soft. I held it to my face for a few seconds, as if I was blocking out the world for a few brief seconds. The smell of the lavender and the fresh towel gave me such a nice feeling; something that had been lacking for more than a while. My mind kept drifting back to that moment of beauty, in the forest with the doe, which now seemed so long ago. I pushed the frail metal plunger down and let the tap slowly fill up the sink with nice warm water. My adrenaline and energy had dropped drastically as I watched the water swirl around until it was sufficiently full, feeling low and as flat as the solid floor I was stood on. I leaned forward and plunged my face into the water letting my hair soak it up. I used the soap dispenser once again, pressing it many times more than before, I filled my hand until it started to spill over the side and then I threw it onto my hair; Rubbing the water and soap. I allowed the bubbles to run down my face and my neck. I used the water to then wash it out as best as I could, making a mess along the way, stopping to fill the small sink up once again with cleaner water. After a few times of rinsing, I leaned to the side and let my hair hang in the sink twisting and squeezing all of the water out before using a towel to dry it the best I could. I took in a deep breath while looking at my pale reflection. After a few moments, I put my jumper back on and picked up my bobble from the side. Now that my skin was cleaner it clearly highlighted the contrast of smells. My skin was fresh with a touch of lavender yet my jumper stank, it was disgusting; sweat, blood and everything else I had brushed against or rolled in covered it.

I heard some commotion coming from the office area, different from before, it seemed more like panic. I threw my hair hurriedly into a ponytail and grabbed my things as I ran out the door to find out what was going on. As I stepped out into the office I found everyone lining the windows. They were placing their hands on the glass and were looking down at the streets below. I had my bow in my right hand and my bag in my left, hanging down beside me, despite my father's advice, I let them go, dropping them beside me as I continued to walk slowly towards the window. It was like I was being pulled by a mysterious force, curiosity drove me and I had to know what they were all looking at with such attention. Edging closer and closer, I forcefully pushed my left arm between some people and squeezed in between them, pressing myself up against the glass. Despite the size of the room and the large windows, I felt like I was being crushed by all the people trying to get a view. I held my ground and then looked down. There were people running towards us, away from the roads and the desert. It was if the city was a sinking ship and the humans were the rats, scampering, trying to get to the other side before she was to flip over. I didn't understand. Why is everyone running towards the back of the city? There are only mountains there.

Cars were driving recklessly through the city; hitting anyone unfortunate enough to be in their way. I heard a loud thud and watched as one man was thrown by a car into a store window; a woman was kneeling down screaming and crying as she watched helplessly. Some people slowed to acknowledge her and then carried on as if nothing had happened, leaving him unconscious on the floor as the car carried on regardless. A few were trampling, while some helped friends or family back to their feet after falling. It was pure panic and chaos.

I watched for a few seconds more, as I was being shoved from side to side. Then all of a sudden the shoving stopped; I hadn't noticed it at first because I was too busy being fixated on the world below, being thankful that we were up here and not down there. I was safe and out the way; then I heard it. I had realized why the people had stopped shoving me and why their attention was no longer fixed on the world below, I heard it loud and clear.

"Ring ring .... ring ". I stepped away from the

window to get a better view. Everything fell silent as the high pitched ring bounced around the room, no one dared to move; except Paige, She was the first one. She walked forward hesitantly and reached out towards a black corded phone sat on its own wooden shelf that was mounted inside the wall. Some closed in around her as others stood watching with fear strewn across their faces. I particularly noticed the nail-biting woman from earlier now had her palms of her hands covering the sides of her face as if she had already been told horrific news. Despite her already looking a nervous wreck her dramatic reaction filled me with dread, the constant fear that something terrible was about to happen embraced us all. You could see it on their faces and you could cut the atmosphere with a knife.

Paige slowly picked the phone up; the last ring lingering on in the silence, then raised it to her ear. "Hello... Eli," she said with some relief now in her voice.

"Dad," I said out loud accidentally as I perked up and a new energy filled my body.

"You're in the city?!" Paige said, clearly unhappy with the news. Seconds later Paige was pleading "but, but, but they can't"

Paige slumped to her knees, still holding the phone to her ear. I noticed that some of the people had already made a run for the exit; I was assuming that they knew what this meant. The noise levels in the office began to rise once again. This was a bad sign so I hurried to grab my things, getting barged by others as I ran.

As I picked up my things Paige shouted "Operation Reset, FUCKING RESET, GO GET OUT!" she yelled It so loud it shocked me.

Everyone looked panicked and was erratic; except for Paige who locked eyes with me, signalling for me to remain calm. We waited as everyone else bundled into the stairways. One man and a woman stayed, Paige pleaded with them to go and she said it was pointless staying, but they just sat there staring; completely unresponsive to her words of advice. She grabbed me by the hand and took me across the other side of the room ducking down below a partition so no one would hear us.

"Right listen up. Eli is at the head office and we need to get there, it's a few blocks away and it's fairly safe." She looked at me with a look that didn't fill me with confidence.

"But?" I said.

"But we have to get there on foot. If we drove we would have to track the outskirts of the city and that would lead us into the military blockades. There are numerous roadblocks along the way. Burnt and crashed cars are everywhere. Eli said that they are planning Operation Reset".

I interrupted Paige "but you told them that…"

Paige interrupted me back "I told them what I had to, what they needed to know. To give them any chance of getting out of here alive" We need to take the streets and pass through a couple of alleyways and subways. Once we are there your father will look after us, they are protected there. Ok? Got it?"

I took in a large breath to calm myself. "Yeah, I got it". I felt fear grip me again and my throat had begun to tighten up, but knowing my father sat in the one place that was safe, was all the motivation I needed to get up and go.

We waited for about twenty minutes for the masses to clear the building so we could access her supplies. I was beginning to think that Paige was a lot more involved than I had first presumed. I looked out the window one last time before we descended. The sun was beginning to sink beyond the mountains; I knew it wouldn't be long before darkness was upon us. We opened the stairway door and Paige turned back to speak with the two who stayed behind

"One last chance, are you coming?" They sat in silence and didn't even acknowledge her; still staring into the abyss with a blank look on their faces. Maybe they were in shock. "Have it your way" she said as she turned and hurried down the stairway.

I followed behind, my legs feeling weak through fear and fatigue as I hurried down the stairs. We rushed around and around just as we did on the way up. A familiar feeling of dizziness engulfed my head, I gripped the cold railings with my left hand to keep myself moving and to prevent myself from falling; our footsteps echo around the dull white stairway. Paige was speeding ahead of me once again.

"Keep up" she yelled as she pulled out of view.

By the time I reached to the bottom level Paige had already opened the heavy metal door and was rummaging around with some lockboxes and lockers at the rear of the area where we parked the truck. The Shutter doors were opened about three feet, I'm guessing that some of the fleeing staff had used this exit already. There was also another doorway left slightly open that gave off light and was assisting Paige to find whatever she was searching for.

Paige called me "here hold these"

I walked to her as she handed me two cardboard boxes of 9 mm rounds and a 9mm Glock; metal grey in colour, it was heavy and cold.

"Throw this on" and Paige threw a black vest onto the floor in front of me.

I placed the pistol and the rounds on the floor

and let my rucksack fall from my shoulder onto the ground. I picked up the vest struggling to pull it over my head, it was heavier than I expected. Paige popped her head back out of the trunk she was leaning into and could see me struggling.

"No no no, put it on under your jumper. Didn't he teach you anything?"

Paige kept on making me feel like she knew a lot about who I was and who my father was. It felt like she knew him even more so than me. She was a beautiful, friendly and an authoritative woman, I felt like I had known her forever yet it had only been for a few days. I couldn't help but think how nice of a mother she would have made. I did what she said and pulled my hooded jumper over my head and replaced it with the vest. Paige walked over and lifted the tough Velcro straps off the sides and pulled them tight before replacing them. It felt secure around my chest and back, it was comforting.

Paige pointed at an opening on the left side of my stomach; "This is where that goes" pointing at the pistol on the floor "and they go in there", suggesting that I put the ammunition into the two small slender black magazines that she handed me. "And they go in there" pointing at two pouches on the chest of the vest "And hurry up about it," she said with a reassuring grin on her face.

I didn't really believe that she was happy at this moment, but I did feel safer and more confident with her by my side and I was thankful that she was.

Who knows what would have happened if I was still sat in the cabin now, alone and clueless about what was going on or what to do. I sat on the floor and started filling the first magazine, picking up one round at a time from the box and using my thumb to push them in; one by one filling them up. I then placed the two magazines in my pouches and secured them into place with the straps; I picked up the final magazine and loaded it just the same. Paige had finished gathering what she wanted and to my amazement, she had turned into some kind of action hero right in front of me, without me even noticing. She too had a vest on and had thrown her top onto the floor. A submachine gun was resting on her chest; it was black and short, with a strap running around her shoulder. She had even put her hair up like me; I had never noticed it before, she blended in so well but there she stood, a beautiful looking strong woman who clearly had a lot more hidden secrets than I dared to ask about.

"Do you know where that one goes" meaning did I know where the third and final pistol magazine goes.

"Of course I know, my father taught me about pistols years ago" smiling as I fed the magazine into the housing and felt a satisfying click as it found its place.

I pointed the pistol towards the floor and pulled the casing back and housed the round in the chamber. It was now ready to fire once the safety was switched off.

"Wow so he did teach you some things," Paige said with a sarcastic chuckle. "Good, listen to me now. When we go out there we don't know what's happening. People are unstable and the military is on edge. By now they will likely be putting blockades in place to stop any issues and isolate the emergency".

Despite being armed with Paige's knowledge, a bulletproof vest and a weapon, I still felt worried. My palms were sweaty, my heart was beating rapidly and my mouth was dry.

"Don't use that unless you have to but be ready to use it at any moment. Survival is paramount right now. If we get separated, try and find what looks like an apartment building in the square. There is a fountain in the middle and a lot of the buildings have flags draped down the front of them. The building Eli is in looks really out of place. It's the only one there that looks run down, but it's not. We need to access it from the alleyway. There is a dark metal cover on the floor joining the building that opens with this access code or with this card when shown. It will take you underground to the facility. There are hidden cameras there so if I'm not with you use this and hold it up and hold it still. Be sure that no one else is around when you do so. We can't afford to be exposed in a time like this."

She placed a black lanyard over my head with a black id card attached to the end. She tucked it inside my vest.

"But it's black?" I said, confused at how it would work.

"There is a machine that reads it. Don't worry, it will work. Once we are there, we can assess the situation and if we need to, get the hell out of here".

I placed the pistol into the vest and threw my rucksack back on. The strap only just fit over the left side where the pistol was placed, but it didn't hinder my ability to get the pistol if I needed to. Then I leaned down to grab my bow. The weight I now had on my upper body made it difficult to pick up. I questioned my decision in taking the bow, after all, I did have a pistol; I decided to pick it up anyway, It has served me well and it may have its advantages. Paige stood patiently waiting for me to be ready, knowing that time was important but also knowing that it was safer to have a more functioning ally to navigate the darkened city of chaos with.

"Have this and then drink this" Paige handed me a power gel and a bottle of water. "Don't worry, its energy gel, used for athletes. It will restore your Electrolytes."

I ripped the top of the paper-based tube and placed it in my mouth. Squeezing the gel and drinking it. It tasted disgusting; I scrunched up my face and Paige laughed.

"Now drink the water". I started sipping the water but Paige insisted that I finished the bottle. "The road ahead could be a long one," she said with a strange sense of optimism and dark humour.

I finished the bottle and threw it into the back of the truck.

"You ready?" Paige said, standing up tall ready to depart.

"Ready as I can be," said with a lack of belief that I can handle myself out there.

"Then let's go!"

CITY STREETS

We walked towards the shutter doors; the light was no longer something we could fully rely on. As I ducked under and out the air felt fresh on my face. I stood up tall on the other side stretching my aching back with my arms reaching towards the sky; looking up to see the vast mountains in front of us. They stood tall and steep while jagged rock and dark green trees littered its bland features. I could see why this place was such a trap; there was no easy access in or out of here. Maybe the way I got in was the only other access point back out? But that was all the way across the other side of the city now. Paige popped up next to me and paused.

"Can you hear that? " Paige said in a now softened voice.

I softly replied "hear what? "

Paige pointed a finger up in the air and waited. A small pop pop pop rippled in the distance.

"That," she said. "It's the military, probably at barricade one". Paige started walking back the way that we drove in, keeping the wooden fence tight to our right side. I followed close behind, keeping only a step or two distance behind.

"What's barricade one?" I said as I constantly looked around with a sense of hypersensitivity.

"It's the first line of defence for the city. It's there to protect us. It sits on the edge of the mountain about half a kilometre before the start of the city; one end of the mountain to the other, keeping us in and anyone else out. It doesn't sound too busy right now which is good, but it is a bad sign that they are set up in the first place".

We continued to walk steadily ahead. Despite the extra weight and the fact we were walking at a decent pace, I was cold and I was sweating. It was a very strange sensation for me; it was probably a mixture of adrenaline and fear.

"How long until we get there," I asked eagerly.

"Ah, a good while yet. We're going to the city centre which sits in front of the city. That courtyard I told you about is full of government buildings, banks, and media companies. It's the real focal point here. Everything is basically self-contained and cut off from the outside world, and for good reason too. Places like this exist around the world and the people who live in them know the risks. They never think anything would happen, but they sign a statement when they live here to agree that in an emergency the military would contain the area until it is safe. Most people feel safe because of this, some feel claustrophobic. Those like me who know a bit more are sworn to keep our mouths closed outside of the circle. Your father and I, we are in the circle. Stay close now".

We reached the road and needed to cross to the other side where we could use the buildings as cover. We didn't want to be out in the open. More popping sounds in the distance, it was on and off regularly; usually a few minutes or more between bursts. Paige shuffled across the road and I followed behind.

Street lights now lit the way as the moon began to rise, an eerie feeling swept over the city. I expected more people to be around, so Where were they all? We continued down a large wide street, tight to the buildings. There were a few cars scattered and abandoned throughout. There was one with its lights still on and the door left hanging open, as the ignition's alarm sounded to inform its user that the keys were still turned in its barrel. We kept pushing on passing building after building. Paige leading with her rifle slightly raised as if it's ready to be fired when needed. I followed suit and kept my bow in my hands, just in case. Paige stopped and squatted down, I copied.

"What is it?" I whispered.

"Just wait".

I watched over her shoulder down the long dark street. Roads leading off in various directions and there was a fire up ahead. It looked like it was a car that was on fire. I could hear it popping and the smoke was rising up into the air. Black smoke that was thick rose as high as the stars that sat above us; more popping in the distance. It seemed too quiet compared to the chaos that we had witnessed throughout the day, and it had me really spooked. All the noises echoed around off the high walls and despite the city being fairly big, I felt trapped. A man ran from a street to our left, out into the road. It made me jump.

"Fuck," I said as my heart thumped against my chest.

He was running fast. I could hear him panting as he was clearly exhausted. Just as quickly as he appeared, he was gone. I was so physically and emotionally tired that every event no matter how large or small made my mind spin and my anxiety jump up a notch. I badly wanted to be safe and with my father.

We turned left to find more streets the same. One after one Paige navigated us through a maze. I began to read road signs and could start to make out that we were still a few kilometres away from the city centre. We slowly and carefully proceeded despite the lack of attention from any other people. There were a few occasions where they passed us and just like before we settled into the darkness of the shadows and watched them until it was clear for us to proceed. We passed abandoned shops and restaurants, their doors were left wide open while some others were closed and locked up securely; presumably, their owners acted quickly as the city started to break down and managed to lock up just in time. If Paige was right about the people knowing the risks of living in a place like this then maybe some had thought of and planned for a time like this.

My ears perked up as I heard glass smash and shatter, accompanied by aggressive male voices; my throat tightened and my mouth became even drier, I could feel the hairs on my arms stand up. This wasn't like before, we were always able to be secure by some sort of building, we were out in the open, vulnerable, exposed, and I felt it.

Every step landed softly, we could not afford to attract anyone, especially not the loud and aggressive group that lingered not too far away. We crept for a few hundred yards as the noise increased; Paige stepped past an alleyway, checking that it was safe to proceed before continuing to push on. I waited a few seconds and then followed behind, allowing Paige to get a few steps ahead. I stepped off the curb into the darkness that was cast from the entrance of the alleyway. As I stepped off the curb and my foot hit the floor I felt panic wash over me, I leapt backwards, falling hard onto my back. Paige whipped her rifle around to face me, firmly placing the stock of the rifle against her shoulder ready to shoot. Full of confusion and dread I shuffled backwards as the pain of the fall and panic set in.

Paige lowered her rifle, a wide smile filled her face as a large brown dog ran past me and off into the city streets.

"Fuck me!" I said, trying to catching my breath. "Shit"; my heart was pounding as I lay flat on my back.

"Come on, get up," Paige said unsympathetically, tilting her head suggesting that we need to move. "We have got to go, we don't have much time"

I got to my feet, drawing a deep breath of cool air that filled my lungs, pulled my clothes straight before gingerly following on. The closer we got to the city centre the louder things became around us. The frequency of gunfire increased as did the amount of shouting and screaming. Paige assumed that the barricade was at fault for those noises; soldiers being positioned to stop the civilians leaving the city. We spotted a few more individuals run or drive past us in the opposite direction; presumably giving up on the idea of trying to pass the barricade and deciding to turn their attention elsewhere. We were still a fair way from the centre and those militaries wouldn't care about who Paige was working for if we were seen running through the streets; they would likely detain us and that couldn't happen. We had to get to Eli without being discovered or the whole situation would only get worse. Despite the fact Paige and my father worked alongside the government they were no more welcome than any fleeing civilian. We were all untrustworthy problems for them.

We were approaching larger buildings now; these types of shops were catered towards men in suits who drove expensive cars. The surroundings were more beautiful and vast, it was if more care and money went into this area than anywhere else we had travelled through. We were getting close. More gunfire rippled through the empty streets, this time more intense, it sounded a lot closer than it had before. I became much more alert to the noises now, being closer to them brought its own sense of danger and excitement. Paige just seemed comfortable with it but I was picking up any noise no matter how quiet or how loud. The gunfire dispersed for a few moments as I walked on, Closer to the walls, and closer to Paige. A few more shops had been smashed and there was a lot of smoke ahead. We crossed the poorly lit road where the light glistened off the glass that was scattered across the road before our boots crushed the smaller pieces into the floor. We stopped for a second, there it was again, more smashing and there was a small cheer ahead; we couldn't work out where it was coming from so we proceeded slowly and carefully. Paige was clearly concentrating more now than she has been before, she was looking tired now, and we both were. There is only so much adrenaline your body can pump out before you begin to come down again.

We walked towards the end of the road where a vast hotel stood facing us. It was a beautiful looking building with lots of signs and flower baskets strewn over the front of it. There were two big windows on either side of a large solid wooden door that sat in the centre. To the right of the hotel was Westcott Avenue and a sign that read "*town square 2 kilometres*", we were close. I could see the left window of the hotel begin to glow; we stopped again as a precaution. We couldn't work out what it was.

"Is that a reflection?" I said softly to Paige.

She crouched down with two hands on her weapon, just watching. Paige didn't say anything so I stayed behind her trying not to make any noise. More noise grew, this time closer; It was a man's voice, more than one. It was muffled and I couldn't work it out.

We were a few hundred yards from the hotel and we needed to pass it, the noise, of course, was coming from that direction. A silhouette appeared on the corner up ahead; wearing dark clothing from head to toe which made whoever it was very hard to see, Paige raised her rifle. I felt anxious; my heart beating so loud I could hear it thump against my chest. They continued to shout and I sunk deeper into the shadows. That figure in front of us was the man shouting at other wn the street; they began laughing too, I didn't understand what they were doing.

"Why were they laughing?" I whispered to Paige.

As the orange glow in the hotel window grew it looked more and more like a reflection. The man was facing away from us as we sat quietly watching; he looked back down the street towards where he came from and shouted

"Fuck yeah, fuck this town... FUCK THE BARRICADE!" As he said this he raised his right hand, he was tightly gripping what looked like a brick; he launched it straight at the hotel window, sending it crashing through its large chunky wooden frame.

As soon as the glass shattered he stumbled backwards away from the hotel, watching his work with satisfaction. A large fireball engulfed the front of the building; as if it was climbing the wall leaving flags and flower baskets alight, we could feel the heat from this far back. Paige pulled me closer to the wall as more men walked around the corner cheering. More bricks being thrown at anything that could be broken. One man turned towards us, I froze. He was wearing some sort of cloth across his face; a few of them had bats and metal poles, there must have been ten or fifteen of them, all cheering and smashing things.

Paige whispered to me "move back. Slowly"

I felt sick as the situation grew more and more tense. I carefully moved back while crouching and Paige did the same, facing forward and never breaking eye contact with them. A few more of them turned in our direction; the fire lighting up the sky behind them casting their shadows towards us. It was clear now that the hotel wasn't the only building on fire. Black smoke billowed into the sky from the direction that they had come.

"THERE"

Paige stood up, pulling me up by my vest

"RUN!" she shouted as she shoved me back down the street.

I ran feeling like my whole body was on alert, my skin tightening with anticipation; I ran hard trying not to trip in the darkness. I looked behind to see where Paige was, slowing down to see her walking backwards with her rifle raised; she wasn't saying anything as the men gathered together. They didn't seem uncomfortable with a weapon pointed at them.

I had slowed down to a brisk walk keeping my eyes firmly fixed on Paige and the group beyond her; a hand reached out of the mass of men as if it was pointing at us, and before I could assess what was happening, a bullet exploded in the concrete wall next to Paige's head; I heard a loud crack as another zipped past me. Paige ducked down and rolled sideways away from the wall, everything was in slow motion except for my heart which was trying to jump out of my chest.

"PAIGE!"

She quickly got onto one knee firing six rapid single shots into the group, two of the men instantly dropped to the floor while other's scattered to the sidewalks; one running off clutching his stomach, he had clearly been hit. Another bullet hit the ground about two feet in front of Paige as she turned and ran towards me; while the screams of pain and anger play out in the background. I too turned and ran; my body tensed as more shots landed around us.

"Fuck fuck fuck!" I shouted as rounds impacted right next to my feet sending shards of concrete up into the air.

I trip over as panic and fear overwhelms me, I quickly get my feet back under my body as a blinding light consumes the street. I had no option but to cover my eyes and stop running, despite the constant threat from behind. As my eyesight begins to return I hear a loud roar from behind the light and the floor begins to rumble. So much confusion and adrenaline pumping around my body; I lower my trembling hand to see a soldier mounted on the top of a Humvee with a large machine gun. It was a convoy; driving directly towards us. I lunge forward with some urgency and managed to crawl around the corner to an alleyway. More rounds scatter around the entrance and some clipped the front of the Humvee; the soldier on top swings his weapon towards the incoming fire and opened up, the noise of each round being fired made a shockwave hit me, each round a deep deliberate thud.

I crouched against the wall covering my ears as smoke began to fill the street. The thought of Paige in danger quickly appeared in my head and replaced the selfish urge to curl up. I leaned around the corner to see Paige running on the other side of the road into the adjourning alleyway.

She turns around to see me once she is out of the firing line and signals for me to run.

"GO!....... I WILL FIND YOU".

"NO!" I shouted back, not wanting to be left alone. She couldn't hear me due to the noises of battle and the loud engines so I stepped closer and shouted louder. The Humvee cuts us off; driving forward and obstructing my view. I was about to run around the front of it to get to her as multiple rounds impacted the front of the convoy, pushing my back into the alleyway, retreating into the darkness, alone.

PLAY IT SAFE

I ran as hard as I could, the need for air was so vast that it was stretching my lungs to new levels; my heart was beating out of control. I ran the length of the alleyway dodging wet potholes and large garbage containers; at some point, I saw a man and what I assumed was his daughter huddled up against the large rubbish container, slumped on the floor. I was too fearful of what was behind me to even think of their situation or their needs; I had no intention of stopping to help them until I felt safe and clear. I looked behind me to see a truck pass at the back of the convoy; they were advancing up the street towards the threat. I slowed to a walk and hid up against a wall, trying to calm my breathing and my trembling hands, achieving either was difficult.

I slid down the wall and sat on the floor; I could feel my throat tighten up as emotions of fear and sadness swept over me, I couldn't believe what had just happened. I had grown up living a quiet life and had been cast into a violent and dangerous world, I just wanted to go back home. I sat there for a few minutes getting my breathing right, listening to the violent firefight up the street. The words move popped into my head, I'm not sure if it sounded like my father's voice, maybe it was what I would have expected him to say to me; either way, it was enough for me to wipe the tears from my cold wet face and get to my feet. I stood up brushing the dirt from my clothing and stepped closer towards the next road where a street light made little difference in illuminating the ground before me.

The light was just strong enough for me to see where someone had spilt blood on the pavement and dragged their foot through it in the direction they were travelling. Suddenly the urge for me to venture out on the street had dramatically reduced. I crept forward slowly not knowing what could be lurking around the corner. I let my hands walk down the cold damp wall to locate the corner of the alleyway before carefully allowing my face to peer around. A body lay face down on the curb a few feet away. I took a sharp breath, shocked and scared at the sight; I quickly scan around me to make sure that this was the only thing I needed to be cautious of and it was. I focused on the persons back to look for signs of breathing which was nearly impossible in the low lighting. Was this a trap or was he dead?

There was enough blood along the floor to suggest that he had to be dead ... right? I wasn't doing well to convince myself. I decided to step closer; thinking about the worst outcome of the situation, I popped the strap that secured my hunting knife and pulled the blade out, just in case. I crept forward while looking around to see if anyone else was coming, thankfully there wasn't; I was wishing that Paige or Eli were there with me. As I got closer I could see that it was a man who was wearing dirty white shoes and dark blue jeans that were stained blood-red; he had a dark-coloured jacket on and his hands were underneath him. I slowly stepped closer with my left foot forward, ready to turn and run. As I got near I pulled my right hand slightly back with the knife ready, I couldn't risk taking the chance to approach unarmed. I stepped again and now I was close enough to grab him, I reached out my left hand.

I prodded his right shoulder; there was no reaction so I did it again, nothing. I gripped his right shoulder by his jacket and pulled hard to my left trying to roll him over. I struggled as his still body was heavy. I pulled hard and as his right arm became free his body began to roll. His arm swung around forcefully, grabbing hold of my bag strap on my shoulder; in a panic I fell to my left, tripping over his feet and on to my back. He let out a groan and two things crossed my mind; firstly how has this happened and secondly I hope that sound wasn't the metal of my knife bouncing on the floor because that means I have just dropped my fall back plan. The man appeared above of me, anger and terror consumed his face; he was set on one thing, taking me out with him.

He pushed his weight onto me; I could feel the wetness of his blood as he released his left hand that was holding his stomach where he had clearly been shot. I looked quickly up to my right, could I reach the knife? It was too far and now his right hand was free and trying to get at my throat. I tried to wiggle out from under him but my backpack and the weight from his large frame was pinning me down. I wriggled, turned and kicked, but I couldn't move enough; I had to make my own way out, or I was done for. I had his right hand tightly gripped with both of my hands, trying to stop him from choking me. He kept trying to lift me and slam me on the concrete yet he was becoming tired. It was painful but my rucksack was providing some protection from the solid floor. I knew that I had to turn this fight in my favour so I waited and timed it right. As he lifted me and slammed me to the floor he was vulnerable. I waited until he lifted and began to turn his right hand clockwise, twisting at the wrist, as he slammed me down I put all my force into turning it as hard as I could; his shoulder locked up and he rolled to his right letting out a scream. I now had his arm locked across my body and his shoulder and face pinned to the floor, without thinking I wriggled my legs out, his left arm now reaching for the knife as I had rolled him closer to it; his fingertips edging towards the handle. I put my body weight onto the point of his elbow and started to lift his arm at his wrist, putting pressure on the joint. He screamed again and I felt him resist against his elbow joint that was beginning to bend the wrong way; I threw all of my weight into his elbow joint and pulled my hands back with all of my strength, his screams were loud but the sound of the bone snapping drowned him out. There was no more resistance as his arm snapped backwards at the joint; I quickly let go, rolling over his body and in one move grabbed the knife. I got onto my knees I drove the long grey steel into his neck, his body jolted and he lay there twitching and bleeding out, his eyes wide open staring past me. I dropped back onto the curb shuffling back up against the wall, fixated on his eyes.

I sat there for a few moments, thinking about how different it felt to killing the doe in the meadow just a day or two ago. The joy and calm I felt before all this darkness; both events with such contrast. One was full of light and peace and the other with darkness and evil, I felt exhausted. My mouth was dry and I was getting fatigued; we... I had been on the move for some time now and I hadn't rested. I looked around once again; there was a consistent feeling that I was being watched. I looked down at my hand that was sore and trembling, there was a deep cut across the top of my knuckles. I pulled my bag round to bandage it up as my eye then drew to my right.

"Fuck!" I said quietly under my breath.

My bow, It had been snapped in two when I had been getting slammed against the floor by that man. I knew it was done for by how badly it had been snapped. It must have been a solid contact to have broken it. I wrapped a piece of cloth around my hand and thought to myself, what do I do now?

The shooting on the road behind had stopped. I didn't notice them at the time but I looked across the other side of the wide street I was sat on to see two men fleeing away. I couldn't see the fire from where I was either but it was creating enough glow that I could see a little cobble bridge up ahead. Shooting from the military barricades were becoming more frequent and smaller explosions were beginning to become more noticeable as well. I needed to move, I didn't know if that convoy would be coming back or if someone would come looking for the man I had just killed. I had to get my knife back, especially now the bow was broken, so I leaned over and gripped the cold black handle tightly. I pulled and it resisted, I pulled even harder and it made a horrible noise, allowing a flow of blood to pour onto the floor. It turned my stomach. I looked away in disgust briefly before wiping the blade on the man's jacket and put it back into its sheath. I quickly checked his pockets for anything useful, there was nothing, they were completely empty. I began to hear the convoy retreating down the street behind me so I ditched my bow and made my way up the street towards the warm glow of the fire. I checked the alleyway one last time to see if Paige was anywhere to be seen, she wasn't.

As I crept towards the end of the street I kept thinking I will be spotted as I continued to walk into the light of the fires; either by the fleeing men that are destroying the place or the military who are seemingly not friendly anymore, either way, I had to keep a low profile. By doing just that it would be hard for Paige to find me. I approached a stone cobbled bridge towards the end of the road, a small man-made water feature ran for some distance from left to right, It was very pretty. Some small fountains spread out and some lights lit up the water; I imagine this I something I would have loved to have seen in the daylight in better circumstances. I looked over the other side to see if it was safe to cross, the bridge was about thirty ft. long and very exposed I had to be lucky to get across unseen. I was just about to step out into the open as a radio sprang into action close by.

It was a conversation of muffled voices accompanied by static. I crept up to the corner of the building and looked carefully around the corner to see two soldiers standing right next to me; they were looking down the street at the roaring fire that was pumping thick black smoke up into the black night sky. I backed up slowly being careful not to make any noise. There was no way I was going to be able to cross that bridge with them stood right there. I had to come up with something else. The sound of rapid-fire in the distance increased as the radio once again perked up, this time it was clear.

"We need back up at checkpoint two NOW! All available, get to checkpoint fucking two, now...."

One of the soldiers next to me runs past the other grabbing his webbing, dragging him along.

"SHIT COMMON!"

They ran to a small vehicle, started its engine and as quickly as that, they were gone. There must be someone was looking out for me, I got lucky. I take one last look around and decide it's now or never and make a dash for the old stone bridge.

I run up over the cobbles and down the other side, slowing at the end so I could evaluate my options, just in case I was seen. I ran on and cautiously turned a corner to obstruct the view from anyone that may have followed me. More jets approach, swiftly passing overhead. Their tail lights flashing as they blend in with the night sky and the smoke from various fires that were scattered throughout the city; once again creating a noise so much louder than I ever would have expected. Two more explosions rocked the edge of the city; they seem a lot closer now.

"I need to hurry".

It was quiet on the streets again. I hadn't seen anyone for a while now and some time had passed. I kept thinking, no soldiers and no people; where was everyone? There weren't even any cars on the road anymore. I pushed on past a few more streets keeping an eye out for road signs and was starting to make out shapes of higher buildings in the distance as the sun finally started to make an appearance beyond the horizon. I look behind me to see the black thick smoke still billowing up from the fire started by that crazy group of people. I guess it had spread through a few more shops and other buildings now; it really was an impressive fire.

I could see a crossroads up ahead and some information boards so I walked briskly to them. There was a large sign behind a plastic window; it was a street map of the local area with a sign that read, you are here.

"Yes"

This was exactly what I needed, I orientated myself to the map and my location running my fingers over the possible routes that would work for me. There were a few to take but it wasn't far, either way, I just have to play it safe. Paige said that there were a few streets to avoid so I was desperately trying to remember them, I knelt down and pulled a pen from my bag; most things in there were now broken from that encounter. The pen was snapped in half so I pulled the inside out, using the plastic tube full of ink to draw various routes that could get me where I needed to be; thinking that I could always go back if I needed to and start again. The next few streets were simple enough to navigate without running into any trouble, I spent the whole time hoping that Paige would appear.

I was now only a few corners away from the main square.

"This is it"

I tried mentally prepared myself to find out one of two realities; either I find my father safe and he is in a position to get us out of this nightmare, or he is dead or not there and I am forever destined to die in this burning hell.

The morning had now broken; I was exhausted, covered in blood and had a thirst and hunger that made my stomach rumble. The sun had risen enough to light the streets clearly now and reveal the true state of damage caused by the fleeing people. The smoke was now more apparent and the smell still strong. Not just the smell of building fires any more but the smell of ammunition smoke and bombs used by the military was pungent. They were still fighting at the barricade, they must have been fighting for hours and hours; I didn't think the people here could put up that much of a fight, especially unarmed civilians.

I turned the corner out into the main square. A paradise in the middle of hell revealed itself; beautiful water features and green grassy areas filled the middle of the square. Beautiful looking boutique restaurants scattered between luxurious clothing and jewellery shops. Flags, flowers and various billboards advertising movies decorated their exterior. A particular billboard read "When there's no more room in hell, the dead will walk the earth" I thought that it was a fitting statement; It sure felt like hell and I had seen and smelt death in these streets. All of those amazing buildings were abandoned; if only I could have seen them full of life.

I walked around the square taking in the sights with my father's building being the main focus, then I saw it, it just made sense to me; the worst of them all, the one where nothing stood out. Next to an empty boring alleyway; the others met some sort of purpose but this one didn't. I immediately grew anxious.

"This is it, the moment of truth"

I find the run-down building and the metal casing that adjoins the doorway. At the top corner of the door is a black metal box. I took a deep breath and reach underneath my bulletproof vest, pulling out the tag Paige had given me. I quickly look around one last time to make sure it's clear before holding it up towards the doorway. I waited, for about fifteen seconds and my confidence began to fade, nothing was happening. I looked around growing worried that all this was for nothing, that I still wasn't safe and Eli wasn't there.

"How can this be?"

I hold the plastic card up higher thinking that it would help, I eagerly move it even closer towards the black box, panicking and thinking the worst.

"HELLO" I shouted as I banged the door.

Nothing was happening; I turned around, away from the door in despair, placing my hands on my head.

I looked up at the sky "Help me"

I had no idea who I was talking to but as I asked I heard a noise behind me, turning around to see a door slowly sliding open. I ran to the doorway and stepped inside.

PATIENT 175

I walked through the doorway to feel the temperature drop, there was a concrete stairway leading down; it smelt musky and damp, there was no lighting in the entrance. Yet this wasn't the occupying thought in my mind, how could it be when I was about to discover if my father was the one who opened the door or not. Was he even alive? I was so nervous, I felt sick. I put my hands out onto the cold damp walls and preceded carefully one step at a time down into the darkness. My legs felt weak trying to support my weary body; I had travelled some distance and dealt with some of the most difficult situations I had ever faced. After a few steps I could see a small red light on a very dark steel door at the end of the hallway, it was clearly solid and controlled by some type of electrical lock. I walked up to it and stood waiting, there was a high pitched noise that sounded like a camera focus and I felt the air change as the door I walked through at the top of the stairway closed behind me. Sealing me in so that all I could see was that red dot a foot in front of me and nothing else. I slid my hand down my leg locating the handle of my knife, once again preparing myself for the worst.

Then it happened, the door in front made a loud hissing noise as it began to slide to my right, revealing an even shorter hallway. It was only a few feet and had one wall made of what looked like one-way glass. It felt as if I was being watched this whole time. Another door opened ahead, In front of me were computers on desks and a wall with huge maps and other bits of information were littered all over it. There were diagrams of the city; I could just about see red string pinned on the map from one side of the city to the other, marked Red one, in brackets, *chokepoint one.* This must have been the barricade that Paige talked of. A wall led around from my left, so I turned to my right to find the room open up into a large office; it looked very much like an operations room. Photos and surveillance imagery decorated the walls and vast amounts of paperwork scattered across the desks. Whoever is or was here were sifting through these things with urgency. There was yet again another heavy door in the middle of the room. Just to the left of that door was a wall of screens that looked like cameras viewing the city, some of which were animated by various military activities that were still going on. The room was lit by red light and was dull in comparison to the bright morning that sat outside. I hear a door open and lookup. Excitement filled my heart as I saw a large figure stood in the doorway; there he stood with a big smile on his face, Eli.

We embraced each other and I was overwhelmed with emotion; I could not help but burst into tears, tears of relief. Eli was alive and I felt safe in his arms for the first time in days. We hugged tightly for what seemed like minutes then we walked into the next room, closing the door behind; it was a communications room with sofas that made a square in the middle. The radio desk hugged the wall to my left; it was a small but a much brighter room. I dropped my rucksack to the floor next to the sofa and slumped in the chair. Eli did the same before handing me the food and water that he had on the small table beside him. It was a dry cheese sandwich but I ate like it was the first meal I had ever eaten, clearing up every last crumb. Eli just sat there smirking at me; I guess he was amused at how much of a pig I must have looked eating that sandwich so fast. I opened a small bottle of water tipping the entire contents into my mouth before slumping back into the sofa. With an empty bottle still lightly gripped in my dirty hands; we spent a few minutes talking about where I had been and how Paige had helped me. When I mentioned Paige my father sat up and asked more about her, I have a feeling that there is more to them than I first realized. I explained how we had been separated and that she saved my life. Before I realized it my talking had slowed and my speech became a slur. I was falling asleep.

I woke up with a headache that felt like my brain was trying to escape out of my skull and my eyes had never felt so heavy and dry. I sat up gingerly to see my father talking on the radio, he was leaning over the radio desk looking concerned.

"The password is contain"

"Who are you speaking to?" I ask in a groggy state.

He turned to me with a surprised look on his face "No one, nothing to worry about, how are you feeling?"

I wasn't quite awake yet but I could tell there were things my father didn't want me to know, even now. I made my way to the small toilet at the back of the room. It was small, grotty and smelt like old urine; nothing but a toilet a sink and a round mirror above it. I hardly recognized the woman looking back at me; I looked tired, stressed and was stinking dirty. There was a used dirty soap that sat on the back of the sink; despite it being dirty soap, I needed it. I filled the sink with steaming hot water and took my jumper off, standing there in my bra, inspecting myself in the mirror. I turned to my left and grimaced at the pain in my ribs and back as I twisted round to see them, there were large dark purple bruises along my right side. In all this chaos somehow I had almost forgotten the horrors of killing that man on the side of the street; how close he was to killing me and the image of the blood pouring onto the pavement as I pulled that knife from his neck. I covered my hands in soap and placed them in the water. The cut on my hand stung as the heat penetrated my skin; water swirled around my hand creating a sea of dirt and blood. I began shaking and feeling intense fear and dread, my eyes filled with white fuzz and I began to feel light and dizzy; I collapsed to my knees in floods of tears and panic not knowing what was happening to me. I felt like I couldn't breathe and that my heart was going to stop, it was terrible. My father heard the commotion as I knocked over items that stood on the bathroom floor. He comforted me until the panic passed and after a few minutes I began to settle down.

He described it as a panic attack, the trauma from what I went through finally sinking in. I managed to wash up and I even managed to find a new black tactical jacket with a hood that was in the operations room, I felt like a new person.

"Ok, you need to answer some questions"

Eli stood up and sighed

"I know, I know..... I work for ARCS. It stands for Agent Recruitment Containment Service. We specialize in developing agents, like me, who are responsible for containing emergencies like this in these sorts of areas."

"Ok?" I expected a similar response from him, it added up with all of his secrecy.

"So what about Paige, how does she fit into all of this?"

"Paige is an outpost asset, meaning she blends in on the ground, gathering intelligence and acting as the first line of defence; alerting any complications to me"

I raise my eyebrows at my father with a look that suggested I meant something else.

"Ok yes, we are... or were, sort of a thing."

My expression now changed to project a confused look. "What does that mean?"

He went on to explain how they have had an on-off relationship for some time now and that last time they spoke he had given her a hard time because she didn't tell him that I went to the store that day. I felt guilty but that does explain why Paige looked after me so much and probably was why she was looking at me so funny in the store; she knew who I was this whole time.

After looking around the control room I

discovered how the military had a sizeable base on the outskirts of the city. There was also a training village not too far away from there that was as a staging area called Oasis; it was used to practice military tactics and experiment with chemical and biological weapons. The fighting I was hearing and what was getting increasingly worse wasn't from people trying to flee the city and get out but from people trying to get in; or as my father said infected people from Oasis. What he described of them sounded like Zombies, only faster. I had a comic when I was younger; it was called the walking dead. I used to love reading the story about the character Rick and his little boy because it reminded me of my life with my father. I only had two comics so I never did know what happened in the rest of the story. The people of Oasis sounded like the walkers in that comic, but what my father described seemed worse.

I didn't or couldn't understand what he was saying to me, it just didn't make any sense. How a virus could spread so quickly and turn people into such aggressive monsters. I looked at the video feed of the barricade; there was a long line of temporary fencing and barbed wire spreading the entire width of the city opening that met up with the mountains; we were literally pinned in. Behind each of the two lines was fighting positions; manmade bunkers, raised so that the soldiers could see over the barricade. They were spread across the line every hundred feet or so with a fifty calibre machine gun sat in the middle, four riflemen and a sniper too. Behind the second barricade was the same apart from the firing positions that were spread out so that they could see between those in front of them. I could see random bodies scattered out into the desert some distance away, one or two close and the occasional muzzle flash on the camera. They looked as if they had been fighting small groups but were ready for a war. The bombing runs have been targeting the location of the incident. Apparently, the military had a fierce fight at the point of contamination before it spread to the military base before it swarmed that too;

hundreds of workers and soldiers dead or infected. If the armed military had no chance of defending themselves, what hope is there for us?

There was a scientific team working in a lab at the training camp Oasis; a ten-man team lead by Dr Revrand. His job was not only to test various chemical and biological weapons but create them too. Obviously, this is a secret that wasn't publically known about or there would surely be sanctions on the government for this. If that wasn't bad enough I found out from some of the intelligence in the room, that they were experimenting on humans. I don't know a lot about these things but I know it its seriously illegal; it goes against the Geneva Convention and human rights. My father didn't deny it either and said it was part of his job to know and prevent the truth from getting out; I didn't go into what that meant or want to dream up what that could involve. It was hard to imagine my father as anything other than that to me, I couldn't think of him as a killer. Dr Revrand's team were working in a small lab in Oasis and thought he had discovered a weapon that he could use to turn soldiers into the perfect fighting machine; perfectly focused, strong, fast and fearless. It involved excessive Adrenalin and some toxin that temporarily blocks out pain. There was evidence of failed trials for many reasons but the document went on to say how Dr Revrand thought he had made a discovery and was sending it along with his team to Oasis.

Dr Revrand was talking to one of the doctors in the room where he was with a patient. It was a bland room with a viewing window and bright lighting. The patient was strapped to a metal bed in the middle of the room and various monitoring equipment hovered above him.

"Dr Revrand...Dr. Revrand" He paused for a reply.

"I'm here, are you ready for test 175?"

"Yes sir, turning the camera on now." The doctor looks to the viewing window suggesting that the camera should be on.

A click is heard and a red light appears above the small camera that was mounted on a tripod.

The patient tries protesting but his mouth is gagged. The doctor with the scrim stands close to the patient, rubber gloves and a face mask on to prevent contamination. The doctor picks up the intravenous catheter and places the needle inside. He looks at the one-way glass once again before slowly pushing the plunger. The gagged and the strapped patient was already wriggling and protesting violently. Trying desperately to wriggle free and prevent the inevitable.

"175 contaminated, awaiting progression now"

The room slowly falls silent as the patient settles into a calm sleep. The Dr Looks at the glass presuming failure as the patient's breathing reduces and the heart rate dropped to 42bpm. He approaches the patient slowly and hears a frantic knocking from the one-way glass, suggesting that he shouldn't. He places his hands to his side suggesting whoever is watching him should calm down. Dr Revrend patches into the room now, no longer through the doctor's earpiece.

"I want you to inject another vile"

The doctor looks up at the camera and then to

the glass and shakes his head.

"This isn't a debate doctor, if you are not willing to conduct the work for me I shall find someone who will. Hurry up before we fucking lose him!"

The doctor in the room pauses briefly, silently accepting his orders. He walks over to his case, pulls out another vile and attaches it to the needle. Once again he inserts it and takes a few steps back. Seconds go past and nothing more happens.

"The patient remains stable, Low heart rate and steady breathing. This really should have raised his heart rate Dr Revrand?"

The doctor looks worried, not so much that they are losing the patient but to disappoint Dr Revrand.

"That's ok doctor just wait. Delta, please lock the door"

The doctor urgently spins around to look at the glass. "No....don't!"

He runs to the door quickly trying to open it, it's already locked. He tries hard to open it forcefully and with his code that he punches clumsily into the keypad numerous times; each time the code being rejected by a deep buzz that offends his ears. It won't open.

"Please, Dr Revrand I'm sorry. I didn't mean to question you. I won't do it again I promise."

He's scared and is pleading to be released; a laugh echoes around the room from Dr Revrands intercom.

"Hahahahaha don't be so naive doctor. There are no second chances because it isn't about your terrible work or your piss poor attitude, this is about development. Even if it does cost the lives of one or two non-loyal workers"

The doctor continues to protest but it's no use. He hears one of the machines behind him sending out an alarm, suggesting that the patient's vitals are in trouble. The doctor freezes, suddenly focusing his attention away from the door and on the machine; before slowly turning around in a state of fear. Patient 175s heart rate was rapidly increasing and his breathing has become excessive and deep. The doctor in a panicked state grabs one of the gas cylinders and rips it from the side of the bed. He approaches the door and starts swinging it, trying to smash the glass so that he can escape. The glass is strong but the door has started to give way and a gap begins to appear in the metal frame just below the handle; seeing this he aims lower towards the bottom corner.

"It's working," he said with a voice full of surprise and hope; he hits it a few times more. The beeping from the machine continues to increase

Dr Revrand is aggressively pleading too "Accept your fate and stop interfering with my hard work!"

The doctor makes a small gap and starts wedging himself in headfirst. The beeping has now turned into a consistent flat line. The Doctor gets halfway through and his hips are stuck. He looks behind to see patient 175 wriggling aggressively on the bed and straps begin to pop off with ease. Patient 175 sits up; his heavy breathing now accompanied by a terrifying rattle, as if his throat is swollen. His face is all strained and full of anger, his gums receded and his teeth on show like an angry dog. The doctor desperately wriggles hard to break free. Dr Revrand has given the order for soldiers to enter the safe room to execute them both. Patient 175 jumps off the bed and runs rapidly to the doctor, diving on him; while he is stuck halfway through the door, attacking him in any way possible, thrashing and biting. The Doctor screams in agony as patient 175 rips into his legs, after a few seconds the pitch of the scream changes and it becomes different, it's now more a deep groan. He then begins to fit as patient 175 presumably loses interest in the doctor.

The doctor violently twists and turns as his skin is ripped to bits on the twisted metal he was climbing through; his eyes began to roll back and his mouth began producing foam. In seconds the doctor was now just like patient 175. The doctor begins to break free from the door just as an alarm is sounded. The bright lights shut off and a red reserve light kicks in leaving the room and corridors dark and dull, accompanied by a red swirling light and a loud siren. The doctor slides out from underneath the door, just as the door at the end of the hall opens. Two soldiers run in and the doctor gets to his feet pouncing towards them, snarling and focused on one thing. The rookie soldier at the front panics and tries to shoot him and has not removed the safety catch on his weapon. He stands frantically trying to get it to work as the bloodthirsty doctor closes in.

The soldier behind steps in front "fucking move you asshole"

He lets rip with a fully automatic rifle at the doctor's chest. Five shots impact directly as blood sprays out of his back, yet it does not slow the doctor down. He pounces on the soldier who was shooting him just as patient 175 breaks free from the room and is sprinting towards the clumsy soldier, who still can't get his weapon sorted. He turns and runs, leaving his fellow soldier on the floor.

"Don't fucking leave me you asshole! Aghhhhhh"

The clumsy soldier throws his key pass at the lock on the door which slides open, Leaving Patient 175 and the doctor to exit the lab along with the soldiers, out into the open.

OPERATION RESET

Sat on the edge of Oasis were two soldiers, Ted and Max; they were sat in a small booth that controlled the barrier for any traffic in or out of the village. They were talking and laughing, with music on; trying to entertain themselves during their shift of traffic duty. It was no different from any other day that Dr Revrands team were using the Oasis. Max was a big strong athletic soldier who hated being stuck in that room and Ted was the more academic kind. He didn't mind it because the truth is that Ted is a bit of a coward. Yet they did their job day in and out. Max sits around and gets Ted to make coffee, the whole while Max tells jokes and makes Ted feel more like one of the boys.

As usual, Max kicks his feet up and leans back in his chair with coffee in hand. He had a camouflage cap on backward and big shades on, the type that could withstand shrapnel blasts. Ted was changing the radio station as they kept losing signal.

"Stop fucking around Ted," said Max with his husky deep voice.

Ted was frantically turning the dial trying to find a station with good music.

"Ted hurry up!"

Max looks over to his right, out of the large glass window as ted finds a station with one of their favourite songs and turns it up.

"I'll catch a fever, it's a wonderful high I wanna go the way of the superstars I got my razor and I'm willing to slice All the way to my heart" Ted continues to sing as Max tries to focus on someone exiting one of the buildings that were roughly two hundred feet away, give or take.

Max sits up, leans forward and pulls his sunglasses to the edge of his nose. "Ted," Max says softly. "TED!" Max stands up spilling his coffee on the floor. "TED!!!"

Ted looks at Max and then looks in the direction of Max's strained face. Ted hits the switch on his radio and the booth falls silent.

"Is that.... the med team?" Ted says curiously as they spot a man in a white coat running frantically from the building waving his arms.

"Yeah, I guess so".

Max opens the door and instantly hears the siren echoing around Oasis.

"Fuck Ted lets go"

They both grab their weapons and start making their way towards the fleeing men. They close the gap to one hundred feet before another doctor exits the building, followed by two more.

"What the fuck is going on" Ted shouts to Max who is slightly ahead of him. From behind the doctor runs out a soldier and another doctor, both of which were covered in blood. Both Max and Ted are confused at this point wondering what they are running from. The bloody doctor pounces on the back of the soldier who was running towards them.

"Fuck this" Max now sprinting towards those fleeing.

The first two he runs past both look terrified and were screaming "Kill them kill them"

Max wasn't hanging around and as he got close to the two grappling on the floor the doctor who was on the back of the soldier looks up at max. The face just as before, fear and anger mixed with a thirst for blood. Max stopped in his tracks seeing this; the doctor starts to stand up so Max raises his M4 carbine and aligns the doctor's chest in his sights.

Max shouts a command "Stop or I will shoot you"

The doctor, who was growling and full of rage,

comes straight at Max with no concern for the weapon. He fires 3 single shots perfectly into the centre of mass.

"Shit" Max says as the doctor still runs frantically towards him. Ted finally catches up and stands beside Max.

"What the actual fuck is that!" Ted shouts at Max.

They both raise their rifles at the same time and unload round after round into the doctor. Max empties his clip completely and the doctor reluctantly goes down. Both were amazed at how hard he was to take out. Max looked over the doctor and sees that one of the rounds had gone through his head.

"Good fuckin shootin"

Max looks to the soldier on the floor as he begins to change the magazine. The brief break from chaos is quickly interrupted by more unfamiliar noise from the building. Two more doctors come running out of the doorway and the soldier on the floor has now also started to fit uncontrollably.

"Fuck Fuck Fuck, RUN TED!" Max screams as he throws the magazine on the floor and attaches the new one; slamming the cocking handle forward at the same time.

Ted is a few yards ahead of Max and is heading for the Humvee; the doctors have got in it already and have got the engine running; they were trying to raise the barrier but didn't know how to. As Max and the infected quickly close in, Ted ran into the booth

"Get back in the Humvee, Ill fucking do it"

Ted turns a small silver key in the control panel and hits a button with his fist. As he runs out he takes a few shots at the infected that are closing in on Max who jumps into the driver's seat.

"Hurry the fuck up Ted!"

The Humvee starts to pull away from Oasis; Ted is running behind frantically trying to catch up as the infected edge closer reaching for him.

"Fuck, Fuck, Fuck, Fuck, Fuck" Ted shouts as he closes in on the Humvee. One of the doctors opens the door, Ted is trying hard to get in but if

Max drives any slower the infected will get in too.

"Get in Ted!" Max yells from the front.

"They are right behind me! Aggggggghhhhh" Ted yells as he gives it everything to get into the Humvee.

He jumps in and slams the door, as it's about to close one of the infected appear in the doorway, trying to force its way inside. Everyone is screaming.

"Shoot it, fucking shoot it"

Max is driving away from more infected and can't steady his rifle and the risk of shooting ted is too high. Ted leans back and readies himself; he kicks the raging infected in the chest as hard as he can. It falls back but holds on with its right hand before climbing back in for another attempt at Ted. Ted tries to kick it again and again as the infected desperately tries to thrash at him. Finally, the infected loses its grip and falls underneath the Humvee; the back wheel bouncing over the body before gathering speed and pulls away from the others in pursuit.

"What the fuck happened"

Max yells at the terrified doctors in the back.

"It's all fucked, it all went wrong" He couldn't make much sense of the doctors.

They were clearly suffering from shock.

"Ted, you good?"

He looks back to see Ted clutching at his right leg.

"Yeah I'm ok, just got a few cuts is all"

Max radios ahead "Bravo six to OP. Oasis is compromised, Incoming with casualties over"

Max pressed his size twelve boots down onto the accelerator, ensuring that he gets to the base well ahead of the infected residents of Oasis. As they get close they see another Humvee speed past them towards in the opposite direction. A soldier providing top cover is firmly gripping a 50 calibre machine gun.

"Thank fuck Max said "that should be enough to take out those ugly fuckers"

Ted begins to slip in and out of consciousness in the back seat; Max spots him in the mirror.

"Ted, Ted. Hay doctor, sort my fucking friend out"

The doctors look at him but they are in no condition to do any good; still frantic from their recent experience. Ted begins to fit as Max approaches the front gate.

Beep beep beep "Hurry the fuck up" he shouts out the window.

The gate opens and Max drives straight to the medical centre.

"Help him, he's fucking fitting"

Max drops them all off and decides to grab a few more soldiers and head back out to make sure that none of those beasts makes it out of Oasis. Knowing how difficult just one of those was Max leaves with urgency, hoping that the Humvee that left before him are prepared enough to deal with them. Hoping Ted will be ok he leaves the base behind in the rear-view mirror. Max floors it following the usual dusty tracks that he and Ted have driven numerous times.

"Alpha 2-4, Comin Alpha 2-4.......... Shit, this isn't good, listen up guys; these are hard fuckers to kill and they are fast, keep your distance and aim for the head"

After a few minutes of driving they notice the Humvee up ahead, flipped up on its side and the wheels are still spinning.

"What the" is muttered from the back seat.

They drive slowly and cautiously towards the vehicle to find the driver and top cover soldiers clearly dead, two missing soldiers from the back and no infected. No sign of a firefight, no ammunition shells, just blood in the sand.

"Keep tight!" yells Max.

"Where the fuck are they"

They look around the area but can't see anything other than dusty rocks and tracks leading from Oasis. Max radios into the base to ask for reinforcements feeling that he may need more support to handle more of these infected, one was hard enough to kill, he could only imagine how hard a group of them would be to kill.

"Bravo 6 to Op....." static fills the airway before falling silent.

"Bravo 6 TO OP!" Again there is no reply from

the main base.

"This is really really bad guys; big Doc really fucked up this time"

Max slowly pulls up to the gate of Oasis which is left wide open, there is gunfire in and around the village but Max can't see anyone; occasional pistol shots are heard from the random buildings before science. He creeps the Humvee into the village, the large tyres crunch in the rock and sand, the soldier providing top cover scans around in all directions. Max opens the heavily armoured door, steps and looks around; more and more firing begins to echo around the village. Max thinks hard about what to do. He looks back at the soldiers in the Humvee undecided whether to go into the village and join the fight or try to secure the exit; they all feel the nerves sink deep in the pit of their stomachs. They disembark from the vehicle leaving the top cover in place. Max and the other three walk slowly with rifles raised towards a staff area, its dark doorway open with traces of blood around the opening, red light swirls in the corridor and occasionally lights the darkness inside. Max signals to turn on the torches as he slowly steps inside. They cautiously step down the dark blood-filled corridor in single file, tight and rifles raised. As they creep deeper inside they find the first doorway that is already open, Max leads inside to find the staff canteen; it's a mess.

"What the fuck happened here"

"Shhhhh," Max says.

They clear the canteen and make their way back out to the corridor. Max steps into the doorway of the next room and stops in his tracks as he sees a bloody twitching set of legs behind the door. He raises his hand signalling for those behind to stop. He begins using his rifle to slowly push the door open. The wooden door creaks at its metal hinges, Max stops as the noise echoes in the corridor and he pulls a face suggesting that it was a bad thing. He waits expecting the silence and tension to be broken. Nothing happens so Max continues to focus on the twitching legs and begins to push the door again. It continues to creak and the men behind prepare to make contact in that room. As the tension builds the man at the rear of the group turns his attention to the end of the corridor, he can hear a low, quiet, unfamiliar noise coming from that direction. He signals the man in front, tapping firmly twice on his shoulder before pointing towards the noise. Each man does the same until Max is tapped, looking towards the new noise Max slowly backs off the room and into the corridor, and he stays still trying to identify the noise.

He shines his light towards is, right at the end is a pile of bloody mess but something is moving.

"What the fuck" is whispered from behind as they too focus their lights on the mysterious noise. More movement is seen at the end and Max signals for the group to back up, slowly. Each military issued boot steps backwards quietly, toe landing first rolling onto its firm heel; occasionally crunching on broken and blood-soaked glass, each time accompanied by the grimace of the soldier. The group is close enough to the doorway so that natural light begins to shine onto their desert camouflage legs. The radio in the Humvee springs to life and Max turns, instantly panicked that their silence was now broken. The noise from down the corridor was no longer a low quiet one. Screeches and screams echo down the corridor followed by the sound of sloppy frantic footsteps approaching in their direction.

"Go" shouts Max as he sends a few bursts from his rifle down the corridor, his muzzle flash briefly lighting the up the darkness.

The soldiers run out of the building towards the Humvee, followed by Max who continued to fire towards the incoming infected who could now clearly be seen. The top cover soldier waves at the others to retreat to the Humvee and he ready's his fifty calibre weapon. Max turns and sprints around the vehicle as the fifty opens up. At close range, it knocks the infected off their feet and the other soldiers open up with their rifles. Max jumps into the driver's seat and hears more static and unclear noise from the radio.

"Bravo six to OP say again? OP...." Static

mixed with gunfire and explosions drown out the response. The base was in trouble, deep trouble.

As the fifty calibre rips limbs off the incoming infected their presence has been made aware to the rest of them who now occupy Oasis and all of which begin exiting the buildings and are sprinting towards the noise of the firefight. The soldiers in the Humvee look at each other with serious concern knowing that there is no way they can take all of them out. Max spins the steering wheel to his left; turning around at speed, kicking up gravel and dust into the air.

"We are heading back to base" A few tense, silent and worrying minutes go by.

As they get close enough they can see smoke rising from various parts of the base.

"How? Just how.....There's no fucking way"

None of them could believe that their base, which was well-armed and well-staffed could be in such condition. They pull up to the gate which is already wide open. Soldiers running frantically in all directions inside, gunfire and grenades echoed around the compromised walls. Snipers in the towers frantically tried to pick off the infected but it was no use, they were too fast too strong and they couldn't tell who was who. It was chaos. The infection spread too quickly and before anyone had a chance to load weapons or prepare, they had already lost. A few vehicles were fleeing out of the entrance

"Get out of here, go to the city" shouted a soldier from the top of a transportation truck. Max could see that the base was falling but was hesitant to leave, feeling hopeless for those still trapped inside. Various parts of the base were engulfed in flames and containers of ammunition were sporadically firing, taking out anything around it; large explosions followed. The many civilian workers and soldiers left behind had to fend for themselves as they brutally got turned or killed by sporadic gunfire. Unsecured and on fire, the military base was done for. The snipers in the tower were in the safest place when the infection spread, until the fires trapped them giving them little option; to slowly burn alive, try to jump into the flames and escape or to end it themselves. As

Max drives off he watches the carnage unfold in the rearview mirror thinking about how it must have been Ted that started it, just one scratch.

There was chatter on the radio and in the distance, Max could hear jets incoming. Two bombs drop on Oasis.

"Fuck!" Said Max, the vehicles grinds to an abrupt halt as a huge fireball filled the sky above Oasis.

A voice perks up from the back of the Humvee. "If that's happening there, it will happen here too. Soon; Max, we have to go"

The Humvee reverses and turns before heading to the city with a small convoy of other vehicles. After twenty minutes of driving, the fleeing forces arrive at Red one. As the base fell so quickly and communications were ineffective, the convoy was unexpected. A newly appointed officer walked up to Max in the Humvee.

"What the hell is going on?"

"Sir the base it's gone" The officer looks at Max stupidly.

"Rubbish, it can't be gone. How can it be

gone?" He picks up the radio and tries again to contact them. Knowing in the back of his mind that he has tried and failed to make contact for the last half an hour.

"Why do you think you've been setting up Red one?"

The officer ignores Max and he grows impatient; tapping the steering wheel in frustration. Max gets out of the car and towers over the officer. He grips the radio handset from the officer and leans in towards him and talks deeply and clearly.

"Get your fucking men together right now for an emergency briefing or we are all about to die a horrible fucking death, got it!"

He offers the handset back to him in the form of a fist, firmly pressed to his chest.

The officer gazes at Max for a few seconds, unsure of how to react and how not to show everyone else how he is terrified of him. He looks at the remaining soldiers that travelled with Max and sees their terrified faces. It was enough to convince him that they must be telling the truth.

"Right lads, everyone behind the ammo container now; leave a skeleton watch on the line."

Max holds the briefing and explains what has gone on. How it started and how a few scratches on Ted took down the entire base. How they must have called Operation Reset because of the bombing of Oasis and soon to be the base. Red one is now up and Red two is under construction. The plan now was to execute bombing runs on the base and hopefully, that would be enough to neutralize the threat. They knew if they had a fight at Red one it would be difficult against an enemy that only died from headshots. As brutal as a 50 calibre machine gun is, accuracy isn't its primary function.

"Shit. How do you guys have all of this information?"

Eli looks over at her "We have people working in the military too. Like spies I guess. As I said, we recruit secret agents".

Max spends the next hour or so detailing soldiers to build up better defences knowing what may be coming their way. If the infected turned the remaining people in the base and then they get out before the bombing runs started then he knew they would be in for an almighty scrap for the city, and if they lost that? Who knows where it would end, another city, a few cities or quite simply the world. Red one was now in place and Max had most of the ammunition brought to the firing positions. As the enemy wouldn't be shooting back there was no reason not to have everything readily available. He could see that all the men were nervous. They too knew the stakes and that they were pinned in just as much as the citizens. They all trained for some sort of situation like this. Yet they never expected to be fending off their now stronger, superior, fellow soldiers and brothers.

Max walks up to fire point one, right in the middle of Red one; considered to be the position of the first contact and most vulnerable. If either flank is lost then fire point one is isolated and surrounded, leaving little or no hope for the soldiers that remain there. He drops down into the position, it's surrounded by sandbags and razor wire that leads out either side; it's steep at the front to prevent any enemy from being able to rush the position. It is something that the Japanese used to do in the Pacific War with great effect. Max slumps down on a sandbag next to a few soldiers who were sat waiting for further instruction or action. It's quiet and they are visually nervous, one plays with his cross necklace and one looks at a picture of his wife as if for the last time. Max kicks his feet out and lands them on top of a pile of ammunition boxes. He pulls out a pack of cigarettes and a black Zippo lighter that has a skull in the centre. It was clear that the lighter has been used many times from the scratches and dents that decorated it. He offers a cigarette to the others and then lights up his own, letting out a long lungful of smoke.

"Agh that's better.

Now listen up, this ... beast is no longer someone you know. It is vicious and very hard to kill. You'll want to empty your magazines but it won't fuckin die unless you blast its ugly brains all over this sandy bitch. Understand?"

The soldiers nod but remain quiet. The anticipation of war is what they live for. This is different. The unknown is scary enough but the thought of a bloodthirsty, hard to kill monsters strikes fear deep inside. A familiar noise grumbles in the distance. Max knows instantly what this is.

"Better late than never boys heads up"

The jets zip overhead and head out towards the base, shortly followed by two large explosions. The men in fire point one smile and cheer as the ball of fire raises high in the sky. A few minutes later a runner appears from red two.

"Max, MAX! We made contact with the birds. They were too late. There's a fucking horde coming, twenty mins out!"

The men in the sandpit look to the floor, some look to the sky. Max stands up flicking his cigarette over the razor wire while looking out into the distance

"Listen up boys, there ain't no point in quitting, no room for fear or doubt. It's kill or be killed. We cannot withdraw because there will be nothing worth going back to. All you have is the guy next to you, your balls and a big pile of U S n Fucking A firepower. You are only preventing the end of the world. HOOAH?"

The other soldiers stand up and ready their weapons

"HOOAH"

Max shakes each of their hands before stepping back out of the pit and heads back to the command post.

THE HEART BREAKS HARD

Dee was watching the cameras as the military set up Red two at the city entrance. It looks frantic as soldiers run around preparing for something big.

"But the bombs would have stopped them right?" Dee looks to Eli who is typing away on a laptop with a satellite ariel attached to the side of it "Dad?"

He is too busy and doesn't hear the question; Dee carries on watching the cameras for a bit and gets bored so decides to have a look around some more, she has her hands wrapped around a nice warm mug of tea. Despite the early summer weather outside, the bunker remained cold and damp, the tea was a welcomed sugary treat at this point. Dee sifts through some paperwork, it's scattered all over this place. The other staff occupying this office must have left in a hurry. Eli places the laptop down and runs into the radio room picking the phone up, Dee notices and gets concerned however Eli begins a lengthy conversation with someone and shuts the door, leaving Dee in the control room.

"I guess I'm not important enough to hear that then" Dee mutters as she discovers a little red file with the words "recruit profiles" on the side of its well-used spine. Being nosy, Dee pulls up a chair and sits to have a look through whilst finishing off her tea. She turns over the cover to find a few pages of instruction and other legalities that do not interest her so she turns some more. *Mr Art Blakley, age 29 from Washington.* His picture is shown in the top left of the page followed by some of his personal details; everything from education information and personal traits to body strengths and weaknesses. Dee sips her tea as she moves onto the next page. *Mr James Witold, age 21 from Sussex UK.* The next page was *Maria Fass 32, Brian Raul 34* followed by *Andreas Maudhant.* Beginning to get bored she turns to the next page, not really taking care to read the many profiles before skipping to the next one.

Something grabs her attention and suddenly Dee is invested in the content. A picture that looks a few years old but looks very familiar. *Miss Daisy Earls, age 19 from Eindhoven.* Dee stares at the picture.

"She looks like me?" is whispered out of Dee's mouth as she scans the details. *Area of relocation - North America, Age of recruitment - 3. Handler - Eli Caldwell.* Dee sits up straight, flipping the pages frantically back to the front and sees the page that reads.

ARCS procedures. Any agent recruited into the ARCS program must be unaware of their enrolment or fully understanding of the sensitive nature of our work; once initiated they must commit to a lifetime of secrecy. If a life fed agent (unknowing agent) discovers their recruitment processes before being fully committed to the program then that agent's contract must be terminated.

Dee stands up dropping her mug on the floor, smashing it in all directions with a flood of tea following. She stares in shock as things begin to make sense and her hands begin to shake and sweat. Her throat thickens as she realizes Eli is not her father and she has been taken as a child and trained to be an asset for an agency that covers up biological and chemical testing. Dee vomits on the floor and tears run down her face. She looks to the door where Eli is, wiping her mouth and then looks at the door that leads to the exit. Emotions and confusion gripping Dee as she flees out of the building to the courtyard outside. She slumps to her knees in front of a beautiful fountain that glistens in the sunlight. Her tears dripping onto the dry floor are quickly absorbed by dry dust.

Daisy hears a noise and realizing that she has now run outside, she is once again vulnerable. She turns to look and sees Paige turning the corner. Paige spots Daisy as she gets up off the floor and Paige sees the tears falling from her face.

"Dee, what's.........?"

Before Paige could finish Daisy backs away from her, unsure of what is going on or who to trust. What did the document mean by terminating the contract? Was Daisy now in danger from her only friends and family? Scared and emotional, Daisy turns and runs leaving Paige confused who hurries to find Eli. As Paige heads to the entrance Eli is running out of the building.

"What the fuck happened, did you tell her?"

Eli looks to the sky and puts his hands on his head. "No, FUCK! She found the agents file"

Paige pauses before embracing Eli. They

briefly enjoy the reunion before deciding to go after Dee. As the pair go after her an almighty noise breaks out in the distance. Rapid gunfire and explosions echo around the seemingly vacant city. Eli looks at Paige expressing his concerns

"We don't have much time, we need to find her and get out of here before they burn this city"

They press on finally seeing Daisy from a distance. Paige shouts to her

"Dee listen, we know you're upset but we don't want to hurt you, were here to help"

Daisy looks back and sees them

"How could you, you abducted me! You ripped me from my family and now you want to kill me!"

With the sound of gunfire seemingly increasing Eli steps forward, each time Dee stepping back away from them.

"Listen, Dee, it's not like that, you were taken and enrolled in the program. But not like you think; there was a fire but you're the only one that made it out, I raised you as my own, I love you. The barricade is under attack, we need to get you out of here. There's a compound at the back of the city used for training, there is climbing equipment there. It's a tough climb but we can make it".

Eli steps forward a few more spaces.

"STOP go away, I don't believe you,"

Paige shouts over the noise "Dee believe us, you have to, we need to go!"

Scared, confused and feeling very alone Daisy does not know what to do. She wants to believe them but can't do it. It's too soon.

Max is stood on sandbags at Red two watching hundreds of infected rush towards the barricade through a set of binoculars. Snipers are lying in fire positions, working overtime, throwing everything they have at them. After a while they begin to close in; Soldiers firing single shots against hundreds of infected while being under that pressure goes against every instinct not to unload in fully automatic. Some of them can't withstand their instincts and flip their fire rate to automatic and begin unleashing everything, as more and more close in on fire point one.

Max stands eagerly watching.

"No-No! Single shots to the head, single shots to the fucking head!"

This panic hinders the soldier ineffective, the infected absorbing rounds into their body, unfazed by them, allowing the determined infected to get closer to fire point one.

Max looks over growing ever concerned at the task ahead; waves his arms to the mortar team a few yards behind Red two. He gives the signal and the mortar teams begin dropping M98 mortars into the tubes, sending them off at a high angle. They were landing ahead of Red one. Five mortar teams spread across two hundred feet continued to fire the mortars off into the oncoming infected; the occasional mortar landing in the sand and not inflicting any damage, others landing directly next to a rushing zombie, sending limbs and blood spraying in all directions. One torso with one arm continued to pull its self towards the barricade, internal organs falling out behind, its face is ripped to bits, shrapnel implanted in its cheekbone and half of its jaw missing, yet it still goes on. One of the soldiers stopped shooting seeing this,

"Holy fuck" The battle so intense no one could hear him. They could just see his lips move as a sergeant pulls the soldier back down and uses his hand to point towards the enemy, suggesting that he gets shooting again.

Max moves forward and stands up on one of the fire points. A soldier in the pit turns to see Max stood on the back of the sandbags. He had his legs wide to brace himself, cigarette in his mouth and an M1 rocket launcher sat on his shoulder

"Have this you ugly fuckers" Max fires the rocket. It shoots off into the distance directly hitting one of the oncoming bloodthirsty monsters sending bits of shrapnel and flesh everywhere; throwing another nearby rampant infected twenty feet in another direction. The soldier watching from below laughs hysterically at Max's actions and turns his attention back to the front.

Meanwhile, Paige has been sat with Dee,

embracing her and explaining what has really gone on. That she really was a lone survivor of a house fire and instead of foster care Eli had recruited her and raised her as his own. They were both concerned about the increasing fighting at the barricade Dee decides to trust them once again and head back to the bunker. When they are inside Eli and Daisy hold each other.

"I never wanted to hurt you. I was going to tell you one day"

Paige is looking at the screens, "Eli, there's no time. Look."

The screen shows Red one and the epic firefight that is developing; rockets, grenades, and anything that can be used from the back is being tossed over. The front line is going through so much ammunition that runners from that back are taking up the reserve ammunition from fire point two..

"This is really bad. We need to make a move. Paige, get what we need and ill set this place to blow. We can't leave any of this for someone to find, just in case they don't decide to bomb the city".

Daisy gets her bag and throws her bulletproof vest back on and stares at the cameras while the others get ready to go.

"Where are we going, what's the plan" Dee looks to Paige for an answer.

"As we said before; our best hope out is at the back of this city where the military train on the rocks. We can use the gear there to climb up and then hike out of the Forest. It's a few days hard trekking but we can make it. We need to take supplies and water.

"Eli calls Daisy to the radio room. As she walks in she can see that there is a wall panel that removes at the back of the room, inside it is an arsenal of weapons.

"You know how to handle yourself and I trust your judgment. Get what you need but be warned. Other people in this city may want to take things off us to protect themselves. It's not just those monsters that are a threat. You understand. It's about survival now. If someone comes for you"

"I know, I know. It's ok. I can handle it"

Eli smiles and kisses Dee on the forehead.

"Ok let's get going, the clock is ticking"

Daisy and Page wait outside for Eli. They are both armed and supplied, ready for the difficult road ahead; Daisy looks to Paige and finally have time to catch up.

"I'm glad you're back Paige. I was worried I wouldn't see you again"

They both smiled as Eli steps out of the building.

"Let's go," Eli says as he walks briskly ahead of them.

A few seconds later there is a small explosion behind them as white smoke leaks out of the doorway they had just left; the three of them now walking together through the streets. Looking like a shadow of its former self, the city is a mess. Fires and smashed windows everywhere, glass all along pavements and paper flowing in the breeze down the road; it was a modern wild west. They had some distance to go before they got to the back of the city but with the threat of the barricade collapsing, they had the perfect motivation to get there quickly.

TO THE HILLS

Max's concern grows as the intense firefighting has been going on for some time. The occasional infected climbing the front of the fire points as expected, due to the steepness of the sandbags they are unsuccessful in their attempts, they simply slide back down and try again or get shot. A few of the infected are trying to push their way through the razor wire, leaving clothing and flesh get tangled up; more and more tried until there was a defensive wall of mangled infected bodies. It was beginning to get difficult for anyone at Red two to actually see what was going on.

Max needed a good view so that he could direct the firepower more effectively so he decides to walk ahead of Red two. The majority of the infected are now close to the barricade and are closing in fast. The soldiers using more ammunition, hot smoking shells are collecting in the pits at the soldier's feet. In the beginning, there were a few shells around the soldier's boots, now there are so many they are stacking up they are covering their feet completely. The infected begin to climb up the front of the fire points once again, this time they have bodies to climb on top of; each time getting higher. Max spots one of the soldiers fighting hand to hand with one of the infected on the edge of a sandbank, the soldier knocks the infected back and attaches his bayonet and the others follow.

Max signals to the mortar team to bring the

mortar fire close to the line. This was risky but if they didn't do this the mortars would become ineffective. The noise deafening as the Battle begins to peak. Max jumps up onto a sandbank to see where the mortar rounds are landing. One hits right in the middle of a crowd of infected sending body parts everywhere. Including the ground between Red one and red two.

"Bullseye, have that you fuckers!"

Max smiles as it looks like that may just be able to keep the barricade from collapsing. Scanning down the line Max can now see a few fire points where soldiers are standing up, to stop shooting and shove one of the climbing infected back to the bottom of the pile. This is allowing more of the bloodthirsty and raging monsters to push up. Growing concerned he brings the mortar fire even closer. Now they are landing ten to twenty-foot away from the barricade. It's close.

One mortar fires high into the sky, it's held up there for what seems an eternity before coming down, influenced by the wind, it lands next to the razor wire rocking it and pushing it all out of shape. It is still holding, but only just. Max frantically waves at the mortar team to stop but one of the teams thinks this is another signal to come closer just as before. He adjusts his trajectory and just as he releases his grip on the motor, he sees that it's not a signal to come closer. He lets the mortar round slip from his fingers into the tube, trying to re-establish grip but it's too late, he ducks to the side and feels his heart sink as the round fires high up into the sky. Knowing the potential outcome of his miss-communication he places his hands on his head and watches it turn slowly in the clouds and begin its descent.

One soldier in the pit hears an incoming round and yells; his voice is drowned out by gunfire as he curls up holding his helmet for protection as the round slams into the side of a sandbank at fire point two. Sending one standing soldier out into the crowd of infected who tear him apart. The others fall back into the vacant ground between Red one and Red two; accompanied by the collapse of the sandpit allowing a gap big enough for infected to pile through. Red one was breached. Looking down the line Max sees the chaos caused by the mortar team.

"FUCKING IDIOTS!"

Max jumps down from the sandbank as infected spread out in no man's land. The occasional infected being thrown into the air by anti-personal mines places into the ground. They have Max in their sites as he runs back to Red two.

Soldiers are shooting those following "Hurry the fuck up Max!"

Max ducks as he runs with rounds raining down all around him and mines exploding behind as the infected close in. He climbs up the front of the fire point and turns around, picking up his rifle, Max aggressively begins taking out the following infected. Ignoring his own advice and firing in automatic. All Red two can do is watch, as each fire point at Red one is surrounded and engulfed by countless infected; turning their prey into another enemy for the fearful soldiers. Within minutes hundreds are through and are pressing on Red two. One soldier has managed to escape from Red one and is frantically trying to climb into a Red two fire pit. Another soldier leans out to offer a hand so he can climb in. The climbing soldier is caught around the legs and is pulled back dragging the helping soldier halfway over the top of the sandbags.

"Help me" is screamed as the fleeing soldier is devoured below, still holding onto the helping solder as he begins to turn into another of the infected's army.

"Get him off get him off. Someone fucking shoot him!"

The other soldiers are too busy fending off the infected that are using them as a way to climb up, leaving the soldier who was helping his fleeing brother stuck in his grip. He can't let go of his left hand to get his pistol because he will be dragged in and he can't get the dying soldier's grip to release from his right hand. They are nearly faced to face as the dying soldier begins fitting and another infected begins to climb up over him. He stares into his bloodshot, rolling eyes as his throat gurgles and groans. Within seconds his eyes are focused, staring back at him while snapping away. His teeth chipping as he slams them shut trying to take a chunk of flesh. The helping soldier realizes that he is in real trouble and if he doesn't sacrifice himself then they will lose Red two as well. He looks to his friend who can't help him, knowing what he's about to do.

"Noooooo don't"

As the helping soldier lets go of his supporting grip; he grabs his pistol and shoots himself, falling back into the climbing crowd, it was too late. Enough infected had managed to clamber on before he had released his grip. His death was in vain and now the remaining soldiers in the pit are fighting hand to hand with the infected. They are outnumbered and weaker than their opponents. They are losing badly.

Max runs around the back of Red two and tries to evaluate the situation.

"This is it. If they breach that hole and Red

two falls, the city is gone."

He stares at the pit under attack.

"Get some grenades on that firing point now!"

Soldiers throw numerous grenades into the pit trying to slow the onslaught down. At the same time, another firing point to the right begins losing control. Max runs back to the ammunition bunker looking for the officer.

"It's gone, were breached. Call it in!"

The officer stares hopelessly in fear.

"Call it the fuck in, now! We're done!"

Max grabs a few loaded magazines and slides them into his vest before heading back to have one last look.

"Oh this is bad, this is seriously fuckin bad"

He takes one last look, realizing that the line is about to break, Max decides to turn and take his chances in the city.

"Sir I'm going into the city. Maybe I can rig a few traps but you realize now you've called it in, this city won't be around much longer right"

The officer looks at Max and nods. For the first time, he is seemingly calm at the worst possible time. As if he has accepted his fate. Max chuckles and runs off into the city.

"Best of luck, fucking ruperts"

The evening is approaching fast and Max knows his best chance of survival is to get out of the city.

"Think Max think. Where is safe. They are behind, it's gonna rain bombs soon...."

Max looks ahead between the buildings and sees the treeline on the cliffs in the distance.

"That's it. Soldiers tremble!"

He speeds up to a steady jog and heads for the other side of the city.

Daisy, Paige, and Eli have made good ground but they are merely halfway there. They notice that the noise levels of the firefight have increased and know that the fight is really on. Daisy looks behind from where they have come

"If they get through, how long do we have?"

Eli shakes his head "I'm not sure, not long! Don't think about it, we need to keep moving"

They pass street after street and building after building yet do not see a single person.

"This is really creeping me out," Paige says as she spins around checking all of her angles.

Dee agrees "yeah me too. Where are all the people, did they get out?"

"Not a chance, there isn't anywhere to go unless they got out on the highway but that is seriously unlikely. We need to stop soon. It's getting dark and we need to eat before attempting that climb. We may run into difficulty before that climb too. We can stop at that store up ahead"

They find the store and carefully check inside. They sweep the building and are happy that it's safe before finding some chairs to sit on. They gather all of the supplies from the store that they deem useful and pile it on a table. Despite the situation, Dee was momentarily feeling happy, being able to get what she wanted and not have to hide it or have it taken away; she sits down and delves into a load of sugary sweets.

Eli looks at Dee enjoying herself. "Make sure you eat some real food Dee, you'll need it."

Dee looks up at him. Chewing away, she

speaks with a muffled voice. "Call me Daisy."

"What was that?!

Dee wipes her mouth after swallowing the half-chewed sweet. "Call me Daisy, I like the name. It's pretty"

Eli curls a little smile "ok then Daisy. Make sure you eat real food please and... Don't eat with your mouth full"

Daisy eats away watching Paige and Eli talk about old ways as they get close. Daisy finds this oddly comforting as she finally feels like a part of a strange family. She gets comfy on the floor leaning up against a wall; thinking about what it would have been like, a real-life, a normal life. Feeling calm and safe she curls into a ball and within a few minutes, Daisy is asleep.

As Daisy begins to come round, she sits up; Eli and Paige are no longer in the store. Night has overcome the city, it's dark and quiet. Daisy rubs her eyes and focuses again, trying to work out where they are. She feels a sense of fear as the front door to the store hangs slightly open. A cold breeze softly and quietly flows through the building. Daisy hears a noise outside, she looks to her blade but is frozen with fear as a large shadow approaches the front of the store. The large figure clearly has a weapon outlined in a silhouette. It walks slowly and quietly towards the door. Daisy's heart is beating so hard she can hear it. She looks down at her blade again trying to work out the options in her head. She looks to the back of the store, there is no way she could make it without giving herself away. She looks back to the mysterious figure; as the weapon slowly and quietly leads its way into the opening of the store door. Another silhouette appears behind the first. Daisy is now terrified as two-armed, unknown figures close in. What has happened to the others and what's going to happen to me; frozen she couldn't move.

The rear silhouette behind moves faster and closes in on the first; the tension grows as Daisy thinks that she is about to be confronted. A commanding voice is heard.

"Don't fucking move" it was a familiar voice, it was Paige.

The figure froze in the doorway and lifted their right hand off the rifle and up into the air.

"Move inside, go"

Paige prods the mysterious figure into the store and proceeds to command the figure. Eli now approaches from the other side, out of the storeroom, to disarm the unknown person.

"I don't believe it! There can't be any chance that in the middle of this hell, the one they call Max walks into my store" Eli bursts into laughter as he embraces Max. Paige lowers her weapon and looks at Eli with a surprised expression. Paige turns and has one last check outside before closing the door behind them.

"It's ok Paige, Max is one of ours"

Max speaks up with his husky voice, standing slightly taller and wider than the already sizeable Eli. "So so good to see you, my old friend. Even in this fucked up situation"

Max lifts his weapon allowing the strap to move over his head and places it down on the counter. He grabs a bottle of water from a nearby shelf and consumes it quickly.

"Max, how bad is it?"

Max looks over to Eli, Paige and Daisy briefly.

"If we don't get out of here soon, there won't be much of anything left. Those monsters are hard to kill and the virus is spreading too quickly. We lost Oasis and the base within hours. It was chaos. There must have been twenty soldiers at Oasis and only one of those things. It was lost so quickly, and the base. Max shakes his head.

"I just can't believe it, the state of it, and the hopelessness of it all. If these things get out into the world then the big guy in the sky needs to rain down some lightning bolts or he can kiss the human race goodbye. The barricades held up for a while and we threw everything at them. Even gas, but nothing was as effective as a bullet to the head. The more we lost the more they gained. It's impossible. I just hope that when the bombs drop they die and that we are far, far away when it happens"

Paige walks up to Max, he towers over her "So what's your plan?"

"I'm heading for the mountains, there's a

cabin a few miles into the woods. We can use it as a staging area before pushing on to the next town, but that's a few days' worth of hiking"

Eli wears a grin across his face, realizing an old friend who is more than handy when it comes to survival is now an asset to them.

"Eat and hydrate my friend. Grab some supplies if you can. We head out in an hour."

Max looks over to Eli "an hour! I don't mean to be a dick but if we wait an hour we will be some rabid civilian's night snack. Make it twenty minutes"

Eli nods. Paige and Daisy go into the rear of the building to look for more supplies as Max and Eli quietly discuss their plan and tactics for the road ahead.

EYES FROM ABOVE

Daisy, Paige, Max, and Eli head out together. They step out of the storefront into a dark and abandoned city. Things are quiet and tension fills the air. With a horde of bloodthirsty animals behind them, the only option is to push on to the end of the city and climb out of this hell. Max leads the line; Daisy stands behind, followed by Paige and then Eli. They are all sufficiently armed and stocked with limited food and water rations. As the group heads out towards the back of the city, Red two is all but collapsed now and the rate of fire is significantly dropping as the enemy grows and the friendly's are forces are diminished. Max is pushing the pace at the front, walking faster than Daisy is comfortable with yet she is keeping up; her thighs and shins burning as she tries to compete with Max's large strides. Max pauses at each street corner, briefly looking around and down the road before deciding it's safe to move on across the street. Max looks back at the group.

"There are hundreds of people in this city. Where the fuck are they all?"

Confused, they continue on carefully. The noise from the barricades has now dissipated into the air. It is quiet and all that can be heard is popping from the occasional street fire. Max isn't comfortable with this.

"It's just too damn quiet. Just like Afghanistan, the calm before the storm. You remember, the time we were wondering where every fucker was, just before billy lost his legs in from standing too close to a dead stray dog".

"Yeah, I remember," Eli says with a hint of remorse.

They pass through a few more streets; Daisy is feeling cold and nervous.

"How much further," she asks. Paige seeing that Daisy is uncomfortable tries to reassure her.

"It's not much further, just a few streets away"

She lets out a little smile but Daisy has seen this before and realizes what Paige is trying to do. Daisy remains quiet but her mind is still filled with doubt. The group have now passed all of the impressive high city buildings and now are entering more residential areas, fewer lights and more exposure. Each road is now packed with three-storey terraced houses and the odd high rise set of flats.

They finally spot a long street of houses that lead to the cliff face known as soldiers tremble. Named soldiers tremble because it causes soldiers to do exactly that. It is a two hundred and sixty-foot cliff face that is basically vertical.

There is a plaque at the top so that once the soldier completes the climb, they touch it, turn and run back down facing the ground; or if on something they call exercise extract, they would then hike the forty or so miles out of the thick rocky forest to another isolated military base. Max stops at the corner of the street and puts his hand up, signalling the group to stop.

"What the fuck"

Max mutters to himself. He pushes on slowly with his weapon raised, ready to be used if needed. Sweat running down her face and feeling very exposed Daisy holds her weapon, squeezing the grip tightly with her sweaty palms.

"In the buildings," Max says, pointing towards the buildings with his fingerless gloves.

Paige looks around "what the hell are they doing?"

In each of the windows that haven't been blocked up, a set of eyes peered at them silently. They could just about be seen in the darkness. It was if they were being watched from all directions, by everyone.

Eli speaks up from the rear with a quiet calm voice "I don't like this one bit, keep moving. The people of this town won't be too happy with the military right now."

They push down the street feeling paranoid at every person that stares at them. Although Max and Eli providing 360-degree protection for the group they both know from tactical experience that they are in a bad spot, easy to be ambushed. They carefully walk in the middle of the street trying to give off a calm vibe, yet they know they are far from in control here.

The end of the street is near and the group pushes closer to the right side of the buildings to avoid a couple of car fires blocking the left side of the road. Max leads them further right

"Be careful, there are a few fires here. A truck is burning too"

The heat from the fire is intense and the light gives off a bright orange glow against the night's black sky, amber's lift off into the sky dancing as they rise. The roaring fires intensify each shadow and each glow from every set of peering eyes.

Daisy feels her heart pounding as they move further up the street and approach the fires.

Eli eagerly looks ahead "can we get through?"

Max can't see yet, so he and the group push tight into the right side of the street, trying to avoid the fire. Max Leans and raises on his tiptoes and can see beyond the flames. There sits at the end of the street, the large steel gates to the military yard.

"We are close," he says optimistically turning to look at the group.

As he looks back at them and wears a smile of relief across his face; a pair of arms reach out from the darkness behind and drag him back into a dark doorway.

Eli screams from the back of the group "MAX!"

He breaks rank and runs to the doorway but it has already been slammed and locked tight. Eli hears Max screaming from inside, gunfire begins erupting from inside too. Eli tries kicking the door down but it's no use, It's solid and won't move an inch. Max's muffled cry is heard as Eli slams the door with his foot some more and then pulls out a pistol.

"ELI"

He fires a few rounds into the handle and kicks again. Nothing happens.

Paige screams "ELI! WE HAVE TO GO!"

Eli snaps back into the world momentarily and looks towards Paige. She's looking back down the street as a group of angry people armed with guns, knives, and bars march up the street with purpose towards them.

"GO, GO, GO!"

Eli shouts as Paige and Daisy run past him. "I'm sorry old friend"

Eli turns and runs as bullets kick up concrete and dust from the walls around him. They quickly navigate through the maze of fire, ducking low under the licking flames and black smoke, past the vehicles, narrowly escaping out the other side, running out of the light into the darkness of the street.

Paige, Daisy, and Eli ran and ran until they seemed clear of the perusing group. No time for emotion to catch up or to process what has just happened. Eli walks trying to catch his breath

"FUCK FUCK FUCK !" he shouts out in anger and frustration.

Paige walks up to Eli and tries to embrace him but he shrugs her off.

"There's nothing you could do Eli. It's not your fault. We need to keep moving"

Daisy calls from up ahead as she can see more people near the entrance of the training area. They too are showing an interest in the area. Paige walks towards the high walls as Eli and Paige follow. It soon becomes obvious that there are a number of people seeking refuge at the back of the city. Many barricaded in buildings and people huddled in masses around fires, unsure of what to do. Like trapped animals, they stand awaiting their destiny. Eli walks up to the entrance, pulling out a device from his pocket and subtlely attaches it to the electronic lock that sits on the front as Paige and Daisy talk to the few people near them, trying to distract their attention from what they are doing. The last thing they need is for these people to realize there is a way out. Or that they stand in between them and the only other safe area. Paige grows impatient and nervous as Eli takes his time trying to crack the access code.

A long way down the street, where they came from, now begins to become more active. Noise is heard from that direction, gunfire and shouting follows. Daisy walks towards it, along with some of the other people who had been stood around. They strain hard in the darkness trying to figure out what it is. Daisy looks back at Paige, worried as the noise begins to present itself as screams and more gunfire, so many screams. A figure appears in the shadow up ahead, Daisy tries to focus as another appears. Daisy slowly steps backwards as numerous figures appear in the shadows down the street. She turns and runs as Eli cracks the code on the gate and flings it open. The people that stood with Daisy begin to run in fear and get inside the training area along with Eli, Paige, and Daisy. He pushes hard on the large steel gates as more and more figures run from the shadows. It is taking too long to close, the fleeing civilians assist in closing the gate. The screams now turned into growls and snarls. Some figures appear, spreading light over the dark road as their bodies are engulfed in flames, which doesn't seem to slow them down.

Large groups of people from down the street also start running towards the gate, now seeing that it's a possible safe area. Eli manages to lock it from inside as the other group of people arrive. They struggle at the door shouting and banging it as Eli backs away hoping that it holds.

"Let us in, please, please. Let us in" The helpless people not realizing what's quickly approaching behind them.

They begin to notice the incoming threat and decide to turn and make a run for it. Some notice too late and get jumped on within seconds. One is hurled to the floor by a flaming infected, as it climbs on top to turn its victim, flames engulf them both and painful screams draw the attention of the remaining bystanders. It's like a tsunami of death washing down the street, sending the people running for their lives in all directions.

Paige calls to Eli "hurry, help me get this on her"

Paige is helping Daisy put on a climbing harness. Screams once again echo in the streets and the big steel door bows as many bodies push it. The other people who managed to get in before the gates closed are scattered around the training area. One has been trying to get into a secure building; one is trying to get in a truck and even a few trying to get climbing gear on alongside Daisy. Paige, Eli, and Daisy are ready to go and have located the carabiners within the cliffs wall. They lock Daisy into the first, showing her how to attach her rope as she climbs.

Despite the chaos unfolding in the background, they make sure that Daisy is prepared properly on how to scale the few hundred feet high vertical cliff that towered high above them. Two of the trespassers have frantically begun their ascent. One of them is trying to break into the building and is drawing their attention to the hunters that circle outside. Daisy looks over to Eli worried. He remains calm and walks over to her. He wraps his arms around her and embraces her, then looks her in the eye.

"Don't worry. We will be fine. Don't think about what is going on down here. Concentrate on the job in hand, this climb. Think about each step and don't look down if you can help it. I'll see you up there. OK"

Daisy nods. Gunfire ricochets off the metal walls as a few of the civilians try to fight back. She places her scuffed and bloody boot onto the first available foothold and begins her climb.

As I climbed the wall, my legs and arms felt weak, they felt like jelly, each time I tried to grip on the wall, my fingertips burned. My toes dug onto any type of foothold I could find. I was merely fifteen feet off the ground and it already felt high. I looked down to see where my father and Paige were, my stomach felt weak. Eli hadn't got onto the wall yet and was stood there, guiding me and Paige up. Paige was about ten feet to my right and slightly below. There were two other people up to my left but it was dark on the wall, I could hardly see them. I pushed myself up a few more feet. Using whatever I could as grip until I found a clip. I would secure my rope and would rest briefly. Reluctantly leaning back, trusting the rope and the harness; two small components that were literally in control of my life.

Eli had just got on the wall before one of the trucks below started its loud roaring engine. It was designed to tow large military vehicles and covered in armour. I looked down to see Eli staring back at me, with worry strewn across his face.

"GO!"

He dropped down onto the ground, running after the truck as its air brakes released and it slowly crawled off.

"Holy shit" Paige calls out as she frantically descends. "Keep going" she yells up to me persuing Eli.

I assumed that they were trying to prevent that idiot from driving through and out of the only safety that stood between us and the zombies, the steel gate. Unfortunately, that was what he was trying to do. I looked over the walls to see people running and falling everywhere, hundreds and hundreds of people attacking each other. Others were hiding in buildings. I could see one person getting chased up an office stairway by five zombies. I was terrified. My hands were shaking as I tried to hold on.

Eli climbs up the side of the truck trying to open the door, it was locked; He was slamming on the window yelling at the driver to stop. I couldn't do anything. I felt so helpless. I was too scared to go back down and all I could think of was how I was struggling to hold on. I felt so selfish. Paige got to the ground and began to run for the truck too. It was no use. The truck slammed into the steel gates. It hadn't built up enough speed to open it properly. The truck wedged into the middle of the gates as my father bailed off the side and made a run for Paige. It was if time slowed down suddenly as everyone stood still to watch the gate to see what damage had been caused. There wasn't a mad rush through the gate as we expected. Paige and Eli stood there frozen. Watching to see if they were safe or were the masses about to pour through the gate and consume them. Looking at the top of the truck I couldn't see anything coming over. There was movement behind it but it seemed ok.

Paige points to the truck "there!"

She yelled as a bloodied, burnt and mangled arm exposed itself from underneath the truck; followed by another and then a few more. Within a few seconds of brief calm, the zombies began crawling from under the truck. It was a terrifying sight. The driver climbed out of the cab and was chased down quickly. His blood spilling onto the concrete floor as a zombie plunged into his neck; quickly leaving to peruse its next victim as his previous victim began shaking and twisting on the floor, he then got up and was on of them. Paige and Eli made a run for a building and closed the door behind them as the zombies filled the yard and trapped them inside. I struggled to keep my emotions in control but knew I needed to push on before I was too tired to climb any further. I still had such a long way to go.

Every time I had to push my legs straight to climb, they burned with lactic acid. My forearms screamed trying to hold on until I made it to the next clip. Sweat dripped from my forehead into my eyes and they stung but I couldn't wipe them. I looked back down and could just about see, around twenty zombies circling the yard; a few of those still banging at the door where Eli and Paige were trapped. I must have been nearing the halfway point when I heard a scream above. A woman was tumbling down beside me bouncing off the wall as her rope unravelled. I jumped with fear and slipped myself, falling down about fifteen feet or so before my clip locked into place. I was pulled back hard and slammed into the wall. As I hung there I looked down to see the woman fall into the waiting zombies below. She hit the ground hard and didn't move. Not that I think she survived the fall but soon enough she got back up and joined the others after they swarmed her and brought her back to life, or death.

My head and shoulder were sore from the fall but I had no option but to go again. I had no idea how I was going to make it another hundred feet or so when I could barely make it ten. Being this high was terrifying and I was that high the noise began to shrink below me. There was no more gunfire, no more fighting; all I could hear was the noise of my heavy breathing and the noise of my shoes constantly slipping on the smooth wall. Clip after clip I strain my legs to push my body up. I was trying to think of other things to distract myself from the height and the pain. Trying to figure out the time, I guess it was around four or five by now. I push up again once I located a foothold. The climb was taking what seemed an eternity. I clipped on to the next point and lent back letting my legs and arms rest. I look down and can no longer make out the mess below. I could see the top of the building where Eli and Page are hiding. I take a deep breath and look up. I start climbing again and despite getting closer to the top, the climb actually began to offer more grip. It still didn't make it any easier, my body was so fatigued. I grew in confidence and hope as I began to think that I was going to make it to the top. The sun had started to rise and a strange twilight filled the sky far behind me on the horizon. In a few hours, the sun would be coming up. My shoulder burned as I reached my rope into the next clip, I only had another twenty feet or so to climb.

I heard a noise grumbling in the distance. My heart sunk as an all familiar noise became more apparent. It continued to grow as I heard an almighty roar above me heading towards the city. I attach the clip and look behind me as two jets fly off into the distance; their lights flashing in the twilight sky. It almost seemed as if nothing was going to happen and they just flew past and then it hit. A light so bright it made me turn and close my eyes, followed by a blast. They must have hit the barricade. The ball of flames filled the sky and lit up everything around it. The shock wave slammed me into the wall and I fell again; only a few feet as I luckily had just clipped onto the next point. I could see some high rise buildings falling and some engulfed in flames.

"I need to get up," I said out loud trying to encourage my body to move.

All of a sudden a burst of energy, presumably a welcomed dose of adrenaline. A few minutes passed and the jets had now circled back around for another run and now are hitting the city in the middle; seemingly destroying the city from one end to the other. The blast once again was deafening and throws me at the wall. This time I fell back about ten feet, ten feet that I had to climb again. I was so close yet so far. I thought that if there was another run then it would have been closer to this end of the city and I was going to die, as were Paige and Eli. I thought this is it, it's all over, the end; after all I went through, I get burned on a rope, forevermore swinging over this terrible city. I look up and decide to give it one last attempt, just like before, one foot in front of the other, never giving up. I pass the point where I had fallen and push on determined. I even rushed past the next clip without attaching the rope; What is the point of trying not to fall when the alternative of taking my time is a ball of flames. I hear the rumble again as I near the top, so I push as hard and as fast as I can. I looked up to see a plaque sunk into the wall, I didn't stop to read it or know what it said but it did make a good foothold to launch me over the top of the wall. I couldn't believe it, I had done it. The jets are lining the city up again and were heading straight for me. I unclipped the rope and threw the harness on the floor before running as hard as I could into the forest. The jets drop their payload and roar overhead, I run hard yet the impact is so powerful it throws me to the ground; I feel the flames rise up the wall that I just climbed, high into the sky.

THE CABIN

I rolled over and lay on the ground, staring at the sky, waiting for my breath to settle. I almost chuckled at how it felt like the first time the jets flew over me as I was lay on the ground; just after my arrow hit that doe. How peaceful it was and how I thought things were hard because my father had shouted at me. I had been climbing for what felt like hours and my arms and legs were throbbing, they literally felt like they were buzzing. I lay there for around five minutes, listening to the destruction in the city for a while before it began to quiet down. My mouth was dry and I struggled to swallow. I could smell pine and smoke, it was a weird sensation. So too were the waves of emotion that flooded over me when my attention diverted from myself to the thought of Eli, Paige and even Max. I lay there bursting into tears, in a forest, in the dark and all alone.

I sat up, wiping the tears from my sodden face and looked around. One way was a scorched city that had more or less crumbled from the blasts and the other way was a dense forest. I looked down at myself and see that my trousers and boots are all scuffed and ripped. As was my top, and my skin. I was filthy dirty and knew I still somehow had a long road to go before I could consider myself safe. I looked down at my leg and see that my hunting knife was missing. I checked inside my holster hoping that my pistol was still there, it was, however, missing a few clips, likely from the fall or from where the blast slammed me against the wall. I had a few food rations on me in a small hydration pack on my back. There wasn't much water left in there either but it was better than not having any at all. I climbed to my feet, my joints and bones ached and my fingers were raw from the climbing. I brushed the dirt and soil from my clothing and set off into the woods.

I spent hours walking in the opposite direction of the burning city that smoulder ed behind me. The sun was high in the sky and the humidity was getting to me. My clothes were soaked in sweat and my feet had hot spots dotted around my soles, I felt exhausted and fragile. Occasionally there were some tracks in the ground, some of which were very noticeable as if many people had walked through here before. I presumed it was the military because all of my time spent in the woods growing up I never left such prominent markings. Once in a while, a tree would be marked as well; some blue and some red paint spoilt their dark brown bark.

I found a small opening where some rocks

replaced trees; I decided that I would rest there for a while, eat for the first time in hours. Again this area gave away signs of prior use, burn marks amongst the edges of rock formations, suggesting fires had been built there, against the rocks to shelter the flames from any wind. I decided that I too could use the same area. I felt exhausted form the amount of stress and adrenaline experienced over the last few days; I couldn't even work out how many days it had been, I just couldn't think clearly. I found a comfortable section of rock to sit down on and eat. I pulled my bag from my back and reached inside to see what was in there. I pulled out a silver foiled bag; on the front, it read 400g Thai chicken Panang. I had no idea what this was but that fact it said Thai pleased me. I had no way of lighting a fire so I ate it cold, ripping off the foil top to reveal a wet mush inside. I proceeded to squeeze the contents into my mouth and chew on its cold lumpy texture. Amazingly it tasted nice and I was too hungry to care. Even if it wasn't nice I would have eaten it.

I polished it off with a small amount of water and then lay down for a brief rest. Before I realized I had fallen asleep for a while. Not that this was a big problem but I knew wasting daylight wasn't wise. Navigating the forest at night was hard enough when you know where you're going, in unfamiliar grounds, it could be fatal. So I got up quickly and packed away any trace of my stay, collecting all of my rubbish and placing it in my bag. I once again set off following the tracks left before me. As the sun began to set, light quickly reduced. Birds chirped all around and this was the first noise I had heard in days that wasn't something of terror or evil; not screaming, gunfire or explosions, it was comforting.

The day passed as I drifted on autopilot, hardly having the energy to lift my head to see in front of me. I decided to settle down next to a small bunch of moss-covered rocks that sat just slightly off the single track. It wasn't anything exciting just something I could lean up against. I curled up against the uncomfortable rock and tried to go to sleep as darkness filled the forest. I closed my eyes but it was no use. The forest felt vast and I felt unwell and uneasy, my mind raced. I found it hard to switch my brain off, at least for a little while. I was drifting in and out of a strange state of sleep. I was so tired and confused I couldn't tell what reality was. As my eyes shut heavily, they would quickly open again making my body shudder. The moon was bright that night and stars started to appear as the temperature dropped. Once my eyes had adjusted to the darkness I could see more around me than I expected I would. I could just about make out the track that I was walking on and see a little bit past it, into the woods. The air was again still and the moon occasionally lit the forest a little more before receding behind the odd group of clouds.

Things were generally quiet again and it seemed like a settled night. A few more hours passed and I found myself falling into short deep periods of sleep, each time having lucid dreams; some involving my father Eli and Paige, some with those terrifying zombies. I kept waking up in a cold sweat; none of this was helping my energy or hydration levels. I finally fell into a deep heavy sleep; I had wedged my hands inside my bulletproof vest to keep them warm and kicked my legs out in front of me, my eyes began twitching behind their eyelids. I remember it so clearly, I was laughing in the courtyard that was outside my father's building; Eli and Paige were running down the street towards me holding hands, both laughing too. It was a happy dream, for a while, until a wall of flames began to slowly chase them both. Each time Paige and Eli ran faster the speed of the fire would increase until it caught up with them. Paige was first, she was ripped off her feet back into the fire as she burned and screamed. Her clothes burnt away leaving her naked, then her skin burnt away until all that was left was bones. She then became dust and scattered into the flames. Just as Eli was about to receive the same fate he appeared at my feet in the forest. No flames stood around him just a sense of calm with the chaos quietly floating and lingering in the background. He was crouched in front of me smiling, holding my leg with a grin on his face. He then slid his hand down my leg to my ankle and began tugging it hard. His facial expression changed from a smile into a zombie-like version of himself. He was yelling something at me but I couldn't understand it. He kept shouting and snarling, pulling on my leg, digging his nails into my skin. It felt so real I could feel the pain, it was terrifying.

That's when I woke up with a fright. Just like the previous dreams, but this time to look down and see a large grey wolf tearing into my boot and ankle. I screamed as my body acknowledged the pain it had caused. I look behind it to see more glowing eyes creeping closer out of the forest. I thought that I was about to be consumed alive by a pack of wolves. I tried to free my hands but they were stuck within my vest, I wriggled my left arm free and used it to pull the vest up and away from my chest so that I could free my right arm. Just as the wolf bit down hard into my foot I located my pistol. I aimed at its head and pulled the trigger to find resistance. I let out another scream as the wolf began thrashing my leg side to side and its pack grew ever closer. I flicked the safety catch off and left off three fast rounds; one of which hit the wolf directly in the head instantly killing it. I fired a few more into the dark of the woods to find the remainder of the wolves fleeing into the distance. I lay there panting and grimacing in pain as the dead bloody wolf still had its vice-like grip around my ankle. His large teeth clamped beneath the skin onto my bone. I dropped the gun and leaned forward placing my hands inside its warm and wet bloody jaws, pulling hard to separating them enough to release my ankle and shuffled away from its body.

I managed to tear off the some of my vest and wrap it around my blood-soaked ankle. It was bleeding from various places but more notably from a puncture mark on the instep of my right foot. He was a large wolf with some large teeth. I hopped up and leant against a tree, pain shot through my foot and leg; I grit my teeth to accept the pain and tried to walk. I remember Eli saying that there was a cabin along this route; a good stopping place before heading on another long journey to the next village. At this point I was thinking I may have missed it because I had been out for so long already and not yet seen it. I walked gingerly as the sun rose behind me. My stomach rumbled once again as I pressed on. Sucking on the straw to find my water supply nearly empty. A small amount entered my dry mouth before I felt the water bag compress as I suck the remainder of the air out of it. The water had all gone. I walked slowly for a few more hours. Brushing past shrubs and climbing over small rock formations seemed a lot harder now my foot was in so much pain. It throbbed and became swollen so much I had to loosen my shoelaces to stop my foot from becoming restricted. I was losing hope, quickly, until for some reason I felt the need to stop. I stood wobbling like one of those zombies, just hovering aimlessly. Completely fatigued I looked up.

There it was, about sixty yards up ahead. Stood proudly between a few trees was a small log cabin. Not too dissimilar to the one where I spent most of my youth. I felt a sense of hope and hurriedly moved forward. Forgetting about the injuries I had sustained I sped up; instantly slowing back down as the pain shoots all the way up my leg into my hip. I took a deep breath and hobbled around the front. I took out my pistol.

"Hello…….. HEY!"

There was no response and no noise. I stepped up the creaky wooden step to find the front door unsecured and easily accessible. The old wooden door creaked as I pushed it open and I hobbled inside. There were two bunk beds and a dirty old sofa, a sink, and a kitchen area. I immediately hobbled to the kitchen and stuck my head below the tap, sucking in as much water as I could. I took my bag off throwing it on the floor, then opening up the cupboards to see what was inside. There wasn't much in the first few apart from some empty bottles and some random hunting magazines but in the last two I found some good supplies, there were even some old rations. I shuffled to the bathroom to find a small mirrored cabinet, inside was a very small first aid kit. I slumped into the sofa; as uncomfortable as it probably should have been, to me it felt to me like I was lying on a cloud, compared to my night's sleep in the forest anyway. I peeled off my right boot, dark red dried blood was ensuring that my socks were clinging onto my cut and bruised skin. It hurt like hell but I got them off. I pulled out an antiseptic wipe and began cleaning my wounds; it stung so badly.

"HOLY MOTHER OF FUCK!"

I continued to clean my wounds until I was happy enough to wrap a fresh white cotton pad from the first aid kit around my ankle and proceeded to bandage my foot. It was strange to see something so white after all we went through, everything was always so dirty. I quickly ate some food and hobbled over to the creaky old bunk beds, there wasn't much appealing about them; a dark blue mattress with a horrible itchy thin blanket. I took off my dirty vest and threw it on the floor then placed my pistol next to the bed. I then took off my ripped, dirty and bloody trousers also throwing them on the floor before painfully climbing into the bed that creaked as it took my weight, it felt like it was going to collapse. I was so tired that I don't think I would have moved if it had. Within seconds I was out, I couldn't tell you how long I slept for but it felt like a good one, it honestly could have been days. I remember waking up and feeling alive for the first time, I went to the toilet and my pee was a dark orange. I drank a load more water and hobbled back to bed, once again within seconds I was snoring away. I woke up some hours later with a hunger and thirst that I had never felt before. Sun was shining strongly through the dirty windows. Sun rays beamed across the room and dust danced around it. For the first time in days, I could smell something other than death and smoke. It was a familiar smell of the forest and the timber of the cabin, I loved that smell. I inspected my foot and ankle and it seemed much better. It was still a long way of being healed or safe from infection but most of the cuts had bonded back together. I imagined that one or two of them would need stitches. It would still be some time before I could put pressure on them without splitting the freshly bonded cuts.

I spent most of the day lying around, eating and drinking, trying to regain my energy. It had been a long time of adrenaline-packed nightmares and I needed the rest. Later on in the evening, I looked around the cabin properly to see if there was anything I could find useful. There wasn't much more than I had already found, but I did find this camera. It looks like it was left behind; I can't imagine why else it would be here. There wasn't much footage on there, a few soldiers joking around in the cabin. Talking about some exercise they were on and seemingly initiating one of them who was new in the group. It was silver with a little flip screen so you could see yourself while you were filming.

I looked such a mess, despite feeling better than I had in days. I was dirty everywhere, I smelt and I had puffy eyes.

"That's it," I said.

I walked straight up to the bathroom and picked up the very small dry bit of soap from the small sink and took the rest of my clothes off, ran the tap with the h written on top. Hoping it would be warm was wishful thinking, it was ice cold. I covered myself in soap and even rubbed it through my wet hair. It was so cold I had goosebumps all over my skin. I threw handfuls of water over me to wash the soap off and get clean. Once I had washed everything off by scrubbing with an old sponge from the kitchen sink, I managed to dry with a rag. It wasn't the best, but it stopped me from being cold. I smelt amazing compared to what I had smelt like. The smell of soap is all I could smell and it was a welcomed change. My hair was dripping but I had nothing to dry it with. I put my bra and pants back on which were far from clean, they weren't exactly nice but I had no other choice.

After a few more days of resting, washing her clothes and gaining her energy Daisy walks out onto the decking entrance; she sits down on the wooden planks with the sun beaming onto her clean pale face. Her hair is dripping onto the decking and all around her in the trees, birds sing their songs. She's holding the camera in front of her as it shows her face on the screen. She scans around the woods enjoying the peace, she feels settled and calm. Thoughts of Eli and her growing up in the cabin they called home ran through her mind, thoughts of Paige saving her too. Even the strong and funny Max graced her thoughts, how he was dragged off into that house. Daisy breathes in deeply, feeling the cool morning air fill her lungs; she lets out a deep breath and looks into the camera

"So that's my story, that's our story, Eli's story, Paige's story, and even Max's story. They were very important people to me and now they're all gone. Everything I considered reality has gone and I'm sat here ready to move on. I guess I'll wander off to the next town, see what's there, what they know. I wonder if anyone else knows about the dark things that have gone on here; if they don't, they will when I tell them. I just can't believe I made it here, just me, after all that I went through. Anyway, if you find this, hear my story and remember my people, they were all heroes, I miss them. Goodbye." Daisy switches off the camera, the screen goes blank.

A hand in an orange glove closes the small silver screen and presses the radio transmit button by his neck. He is covered head to toe in an orange and yellow biohazard suit.

"We have a breach"

In a board room, the transmission is received. Cameras fill one wall and certificates and military plaques fill another; a man in a black suit is sat by a large oak table and looks concerned. He reaches down and presses a button on a communications device that wears a label that reads ARCS.

"One of the infected?"

"No sir, not the infected, it's worse"

"Worse? What the fuck, what is it?"

"Some woman, she knows everything. The virus, how it happened, operation reset. Everything......"

"Well what's the problem, bring her in"

"Sorry sir, it's not that simple. She left a recording. She's moved on and she's going to leak if we don't stop her... That's not all sir"

"What else..."

"She knows Eli, she is his asset"

The man in the suit looks across the table and angrily expresses his concern.

"You know what this means, don't you? We have to terminate her. Fuck me, this cannot get out! It would end us......... Do you understand?"

Eli looks back at the man, drops his head down in disappointment and reluctantly replies

"I understand"

The end.

ABOUT THE AUTHOR

If you head over to the website www.CJAggett.wixsite.com/Deep you can access additional content and an alternate ending! I hope you have enjoyed reading this book as much as I have had writing it. Please leave a review so that I may continue to develop Daisy's story, you are also welcome to submit fan art.

(©) Christopher Aggett 2019.

Printed in Great Britain
by Amazon